Follow the bestselling adventures for teen readers . . .

HEIRS OF THE FORCE

The New York Times bestselling debut of the young Jedi Knights! Their training begins . . .

SHADOW ACADEMY

The dark side of the Force has a new training ground: the Shadow Academy!

THE LOST ONES

An old friend of the twins could be the perfect candidate for the Shadow Academy!

LIGHTSABERS

At last, the time has come for the young Jedi Knights to build their weapons . . .

DARKEST KNIGHT

The Dark Jedi student Zekk must face his old friends Jacen and Jaina—once and for all.

JEDI UNDER SIEGE

The final battle between Luke Skywalker's Jedi academy and the evil Shadow Academy . . .

And don't miss the new dangers, new enemies, and new adventures in . . .

SHARDS OF ALDERAAN

While visiting the remains of their mother's homeworld, Jacen and Jaina encounter a long-lost enemy of the Solo family . . .

P9-CRD-145

ABOUT THE AUTHORS

KEVIN J. ANDERSON and his wife, **REBECCA MOESTA**, have been involved in many STAR WARS projects. Together, they are writing the eleven volumes of the YOUNG JEDI KNIGHTS saga for young adults, as well as creating the JUNIOR JEDI KNIGHTS series for younger readers. Rebecca Moesta is also writing the second trilogy of JUNIOR JEDI KNIGHTS adventures.

Kevin J. Anderson is the author of the STAR WARS: JEDI ACADEMY trilogy, the novel *Darksaber*, and the comic series THE SITH WAR and THE GOLDEN AGE OF THE SITH for Dark Horse comics. He has written many other novels, including two based on *The X-Files* television show. He has edited three STAR WARS anthologies: *Tales from the Mos Eisley Cantina*, in which Rebecca Moesta has a story; *Tales from Jabba's Palace*; and *Tales of the Bounty Hunters*.

For more information about the authors, visit their Web site at

http://www.wordfire.com

STAR
YOUNG JEDI KNIGHTS
WARS®

D I V E R S I T Y   A L L I A N C E

KEVIN J. ANDERSON
and REBECCA MOESTA

BOULEVARD BOOKS, NEW YORK

STAR WARS: YOUNG JEDI KNIGHTS:
DIVERSITY ALLIANCE

A Boulevard Book / published by arrangement with
Lucasfilm Ltd.

PRINTING HISTORY
Boulevard edition / April 1997

The Putnam Berkley World Wide Web site address is
http://www.berkley.com/berkley

Make sure to check out *PB Plug*, the science
fiction/fantasy newsletter, at
http://www.pbplug.com

ISBN: 1-57297-234-3

BOULEVARD
Boulevard Books are published by The Berkley Publishing Group,
200 Madison Avenue, New York, New York 10016.
BOULEVARD and its logo are trademarks
belonging to Berkley Publishing Corporation.

PRINTED IN THE UNITED STATES OF AMERICA

10 9 8 7 6 5 4 3 2

To Steve Sansweet,
a fellow Star Wars enthusiast from day one,
for your friendship and
for helping us keep our sense of humor

acknowledgments

Writing each volume of the Young Jedi Knights requires a lot of help from many different people—Sue Rostoni, Allan Kausch, and Lucy Wilson at Lucasfilm Licensing; Ginjer Buchanan and Jessica Faust at Boulevard Books; A. C. Crispin for helping us create Raynar's parents; Lillie E. Mitchell, Catherine Ulatowski, Katie Tyree, and Angela Kato at WordFire, Inc.; and Jonathan Cowan, our first test-reader.

A special thanks to all of the fans and devoted readers who have enjoyed this series so much and urged us to tell the further adventures of Jacen, Jaina, Tenel Ka, and Lowbacca. Your enthusiasm and support give us the energy we need to write these stories.

1

THE RAGTAG GROUP of ships drifted through space, maintaining silence, broadcasting no telltale signal that could give away their location.

This assortment of merchant vessels, scout cruisers, and security ships had been cobbled together over the course of two decades by the noble Thul family of Alderaan to form a trading fleet. Since most of the family had been off-planet when Alderaan was destroyed, the Thuls had moved to Coruscant, the commercial and governmental center of the galaxy. Through shrewd investments, they had built the remnants of their ancient wealth into Bornaryn Trading, a powerful galactic company with a steady flow of cargo and burgeoning business on countless routes.

At the moment, though, the merchant fleet had no known destination.

The vessels huddled close together in an empty space between the stars, keeping themselves safe. Security starfighters flitted protectively along the edges of the convoy, while the other craft clustered in the center like a school of nervous glimmerfish.

On the *Tradewyn*, the flagship of the Bornaryn fleet, Aryn Dro Thul stood proudly on the observation deck. She wore a simple gown of midnight blue shot with silver that complemented her braided chestnut hair. A sash of scarlet, yellow, orange, and purple was tied loosely about her waist. Though slight of build, Aryn projected an air of dignity that often fooled those she met into thinking her a tall woman. As she stared through the main windowport, her intelligent blue eyes kept watch on the cargo vessels, fleet skimmers, security shuttles, and scout drones she and Bornan Thul had assembled for their business.

Now, with the disappearance of her husband, all responsibility for Bornaryn Trading rested on her shoulders. Aryn turned to her brother-in-law, who stood beside her on the deck of the *Tradewyn*. Tyko Thul was a powerful merchant who had made his fortune in droid manufacturing. Though he was a calculating and sometimes pompous man, she was glad of his support during this time of crisis.

"Is there any word yet on my husband?" Aryn asked. "A coded message perhaps? We must find some trace of him soon."

Tyko scratched his short blond hair with one hand, and his shrewd hazel eyes narrowed in concentration. "No, Aryn—there's been no sign of Bornan. He has simply disappeared." A frown creased his round face, so deeply that furrows appeared in his rosy cheeks and his chin. "I don't know if this is a new kind of scam he's pulling, or what he hopes to gain . . . but I wish he'd make some sort of contact with us."

Aryn paced the deck of the flagship, looking out the broad windowports at two of the heavily armed security starfighters dashing back and forth, crisscrossing the convoy perimeter to guard against external attack.

"You're so skeptical, Tyko," she said. "I don't think it's anything of the sort. Bornan's been kidnapped, or hurt . . . or even killed."

Tyko shook his head. "*I'm* being skeptical? At least I'm thinking he might still be alive and all right. I know my brother, Aryn. He's probably run across something valuable and wants to keep it all for himself."

"Not Bornan," Aryn said, her blue eyes flashing with anger. "I'm positive that someone has taken him, and I'm certain we're all in danger. The whole family."

Tyko placed a fleshy hand on his sister-in-law's shoulder, squeezing it in a vain attempt to reassure her. "If I didn't believe you might be right, Aryn, I'd never have left Mechis III to be here with you. It's taken me a long time to get the droid manufacturing facilities up and running there again, you know. I think they're all fully functional now. That strange programming glitch Mechis III suffered during Imperial days has been completely purged from the system, so I suppose my assistants can handle it—for the moment." He gave her a small smile. "I'd rather be here with you and the fleet . . . where it's safe."

Tyko went to a console to study their random flight path as one of the private security guards marched onto the observation deck. "Excuse me, Lady Aryn," the guard said, clearing his throat. "We've been at these coordinates for as long as we feel it's advisable."

She sighed. "Thank you, Kusk. Time for another hyperspace jump, then?"

Kusk nodded. "Yes, if you intend to keep the location of our fleet absolutely secret. We are currently at risk if we stay here."

"Not just yet." Aryn turned to Tyko, folding her slender hands together. She pressed her pale lips into a grim line. Her husband had always said he could tell when she had made up her mind and did not intend to change it. "I feel uncomfortable knowing that my son Raynar is out in the open. Perhaps he is in danger."

Tyko gave a dismissive wave. "He's safe enough at the Jedi academy. Luke Skywalker wouldn't dare let any harm come to him."

"No one can protect my son better than I can," Aryn insisted. "I'm going to contact Yavin 4. I'll ask Raynar to come to our fleet, so we can all be together. I want him where I can see him, at least until this whole . . . situation is over."

Tyko blew air between his generous lips and shook his head wearily. "Skywalker can protect him with the Force. I'm sure he's quite reliable."

"Yes, he is," Aryn said. "That's why I'll request that the Jedi Master personally escorts Raynar safely to our fleet."

Tyko knew when to give up his objections. "All right," he said. "It'll be good to have the whole family together again."

Aryn looked at him sternly. "The whole family won't be together again until my husband is found."

"Oh yes. Yes, of course," Tyko said. "I forgot about that."

Aryn turned to the security guard, who was still waiting patiently at the door to the observation deck. "Plot a new course, Kusk," she said, "and prepare to launch our fleet into hyperspace—but first establish a communications link to the Jedi academy. I need to speak directly with Master Luke Skywalker."

After a hard day of studies, meditation, and training exercises, Jacen Solo left the

Great Temple and went off into the dense jungle to be by himself. His sister Jaina and their Wookiee friend Lowbacca were busy working on the *Rock Dragon*, tinkering with the Hapan passenger cruiser's engines—not so much because the ship needed the work, but because the two mechanically inclined young Jedi Knights enjoyed the tinkering.

Tenel Ka, who technically owned the ship, preferred instead to be out running, doing her exercises, toning up her body and keeping her muscles at their peak performance. Ever since she had lost her arm in a lightsaber dueling accident, Tenel Ka had taken to swimming in the river as often as she could.

Jacen loved to spend time with the warrior girl, but he couldn't keep up with her calisthenics. Instead, he preferred to go off into the jungle, because it gave him an opportunity to look for interesting plants or insects or animals—specimens he could take back and keep in the small menagerie of pets he studied and then set free. Back in his quarters, in an incubator built by Jaina, he also carefully nurtured the fertilized gort egg his father had given him.

Soon, he thought, the precious egg would hatch, and he would have an unusual pet.

For now, though, he walked through the underbrush in search of various colors of the polished button beetles. He had discovered a nearly intact nest under some broken rocks blasted from the Great Temple during the recent Shadow Academy attack, and he wanted to complete his collection of specimens.

Instead, as he parted a stand of tall ferns and stepped into a clearing, Jacen saw another young Jedi trainee, Raynar, sitting alone on a rock. He found this quite unusual, since the young man usually avoided the jungles, preferring to remain inside more "civilized" areas. Raynar's brightly colored robes were as multihued and iridescent as an entire swarm of button beetles. He sat with his hands on his robed knees.

Jacen grinned and waved—he'd been working harder at being friendly to Raynar since the boy's family problems had begun. "Hi, Raynar. What are you doing?"

Raynar turned, startled by Jacen's arrival. "Nothing."

Jacen laughed. "There's usually a lot

more than nothing going on when someone says 'nothing.'"

"All right," Raynar said with a sigh. "I was meditating . . . using the Force to reach out with my mind. I thought maybe I could find out something about where my father went."

"Still no word, then?" Jacen asked.

Sadly, the blond-haired boy shook his head and stared down at his hands. Though New Republic Security Forces and the bounty hunter Boba Fett—and who knew how many others—were searching the galaxy for him, Bornan Thul had not been found.

Jacen felt uncomfortable when someone else was in trouble or dejected and there was nothing he could *do* about it. Although he often resorted to telling jokes, he knew this was probably not a good time to try that. "I wish there was something we could do to help," he said.

"If I can think of something, I'll definitely ask you, then," Raynar answered, looking slightly relieved, though not too hopeful. He forced a smile. A small one . . . but it was a smile nevertheless.

• • •

When Jacen and Raynar returned together to the Great Temple, the workers had just finished restoring part of the hangar bay that had collapsed during the Imperial attack. New Republic engineers had pitched in with the large-scale work, while military ships hovered in orbit over the jungle moon to protect against any further attacks from space.

Arms crossed over his chest, Luke Skywalker leaned against the *Rock Dragon* and watched Jacen and Raynar as they approached. Jaina and Lowbacca sat beside the repaired passenger shuttle.

Jacen waved. "Hi, Uncle Luke."

"I've got a message from Raynar's mother," Luke said.

The boy from Alderaan instantly perked up and hurried over. "What is it?" Raynar asked. "Is there news?"

"Not exactly," Luke said. "But she would like me to escort you to her fleet so you can be together during the search for your father. She thinks it's best for your personal safety."

"The fleet? Well, well, well . . ." Raynar frowned. "But how would I get there? If we're worried that someone will try to kidnap me as well as my father, I can't just—"

"I guess we could take you," Jacen said. "The *Rock Dragon* looks like a normal ship, so nobody would suspect anything."

"Thanks for offering," Luke said, "but I'm afraid Raynar's mother was quite insistent: I have to escort him *personally*. The *Shadow Chaser* has quantum armor to shield us from any attack, and I can help guard him with my Jedi skills."

"But what am I supposed to do when I get there?" the young man said, tugging at his colorful robes. "I need to continue my Jedi training and develop my skills. I can't be of any help to my father if I'm stuck in isolation with the fleet."

"Hey, we could go along, Uncle Luke," Jacen suggested, still trying to find a way to help. "We'll work on our exercises together. Besides, Raynar needs friends with him right now."

Raynar looked at Jacen skeptically, and then at the other young Jedi Knights. "You'd do that—you'd all come along with me?"

"This is a fact," Tenel Ka said.

"Sure," Jaina said. "We haven't always

been very friendly to you, but maybe this is a good time to change that."

Lowie rumbled his enthusiastic endorsement of the plan.

"I think that's a terrific idea," Luke said.

"Good," Jaina answered, slamming an access hatch on the outside of the *Rock Dragon* and fastening it. "Then what are we waiting for?"

Lowbacca growled a comment, and Jaina nodded. "The *Rock Dragon*'s ready to go when the rest of you are."

2

ON THE HELLISH world of Ryloth, half of the planet broiled under sunlight hot enough to soften rock, while the other side crackled with a cold so intense it would make a glacier shiver.

The Twi'leks, the only sentient beings ever to make a long-term home there, had settled in the narrow band of shadow between daylight and darkness. In this twilight region, surface temperatures above ground remained hospitable enough to support life, but the Twi'leks preferred to build shelters by burrowing into the mountain ranges. They'd carved great warrens, cities beneath the ground, where their clan system had evolved into a complex male-dominated political structure that had remained unchanged for thousands of years.

Until the Twi'lek woman Nolaa Tarkona had implemented sweeping changes through a swift wave of bloodshed.

Forming the Diversity Alliance had been her key to freedom and power. She was the political movement's outspoken and charismatic leader, uniting downtrodden alien species that had suffered for so long under human domination.

Now Nolaa held the deepest, most defensible chambers beneath the mountains, and had set up her headquarters there. After her rise to power, her followers had excavated an underground spaceport adjacent to the grotto that allowed her powerful allies direct access to Ryloth, and from there, out to the galaxy at large.

The Twi'lek leader sat in her cool, expanded grotto, a throne room of sorts. She had a great deal of work to do. Managing a galaxy-wide political movement required constant effort, concentration, and vigilance.

Here, deep underground, she had to rely on chronometers and assistants to tell her when it was time to stop working and begin the sleeping period. Of late, though, she had curtailed her rest hours. Plans she had set in motion continued to brew; their demands weighed heavily upon her, and she had far too many obligations to bother with sleep. If her revolution failed and she was killed, then she could sleep for all eternity.

Nolaa sat comfortably in her stone chair, not allowing the seething thoughts and emotions inside to show though her facade of outward calm. In a sense, the rich red lighting in this room spoke for her. It reflected the deep-seated anger and thirst for revenge that boiled in her heart, and the multitude of ideas for bringing about the ultimate triumph of the Diversity Alliance that whirled through her mind.

She clacked her finger claws together, feeling their tough hardness, like the spines on the shell of a sidrek megapede. Nolaa could rip out the throat of any enemy—or unsuspecting friend—with one sweep of her hands. Although she kept herself physically ready for combat, her primary arsenal consisted of the *words* she used to forge the emotions of crowds into weapons, turning her followers into a fighting force. Nolaa Tarkona had become good at getting her way.

Hovrak, her wolfman Adjutant Advisor,

marched into the room, his feral eyes bright in the grotto dimness. Nolaa kept the reddish lights turned down, but her rose-quartz eyes focused well in the shadows. She could see that he bore a dispatch in his hairy paw.

With his other hand Hovrak brushed down the dark brown fur that bristled on his face. He bared his teeth in a gesture of respect and said, "Esteemed Tarkona, I have excellent news—dispatches from two more candidate worlds."

"Good." Nolaa bowed her head, twitching her one remaining head-tail in satisfaction. The burned stump of the other jiggled in a reflex of long-remembered pain.

Hovrak kept a long and detailed list on an electronic datapad, recording all known nonhuman species. It was his intent—and hers—to recruit members from each one of those species for the Diversity Alliance.

"First off," the wolfman said, speaking in a sharp voice, as if trying to bite off each word as it emerged from his mouth, "we have a pledge from a self-appointed United Council of Bith Musicians. They have sworn to play patriotic songs that espouse the goals of the Diversity Alliance while they tour the planets of the galaxy."

"Songs?" Nolaa said, allowing a frown to crease her forehead. "We need soldiers and fighters willing to die for our cause—not minstrels."

"If I might point out, Esteemed Tarkona, the potential payoffs of dispersing propaganda. One song to the right audience in the right cantina in the right town could result in riots . . . even the overthrow of a long-established human government. At the very least, it will increase awareness of what the Diversity Alliance stands for."

"Very well," Nolaa said, "just so long as these musicians don't demand excessive payment. What else?"

"We received a messenger from a sub-hive of the Bartokk species. They are renowned killers, assassins who travel together sharing a single mind. This sub-hive has sworn allegiance to the Diversity Alliance—and as you know, when one of them agrees, they *all* agree."

Nolaa Tarkona tapped her claws together. "That's much better news. So, does this mean the entire Bartokk homeworld is ours? Is this sub-hive the legitimate government there?"

"No, Esteemed Tarkona, but they will

carry our message far and wide. In fact, as I understand their species, if this sub-hive assassinated key members in other sub-hives, they could absorb all those minds into an even larger swarm. Given a little time and a little ingenuity, our one sub-hive could subsume all other Bartokks and incorporate them into one giant fighting force that would be completely loyal to us."

Now the Twi'lek woman smiled, showing her pointed teeth. "Very good, indeed. Governments operate by the will of the populace. We make our own legitimacy."

"Yes," Hovrak snarled, "legitimacy. Payback time. By rights the galaxy should be ours."

"Now, don't get greedy," Nolaa said. "At least not so soon. A few sectors at a time should be enough . . . for the moment." She twitched her head-tail, feeling a tingle of sensation. "I just received word that a ship has docked at our underground facility. I believe it is Boba Fett, returned to us. Go and bring him here. I wish to see what our bounty hunter has retrieved for me."

Hovrak bared his teeth again, then spun about and padded out of the grotto.

Putting her nervous energy to use, Nolaa reached out and selected a sharp durasteel file from the small obsidian pedestal beside her. She inserted the tool into her mouth and briskly filed her front teeth to maintain their pointed tips and razor-sharp edges. She received a delicious, forbidden thrill in doing so. Twi'lek female slaves traditionally had their teeth sanded flat to keep them from biting their masters, and only the vicious males had been allowed to flaunt their fangs. Until now.

The degraded females found themselves powerless and sold into slavery, forced to serve or dance—mere objects to be beaten and sacrificed at the whim of their masters. Nolaa knew this all too well: her own half-sister had paid the ultimate price. But she had vowed to change all that. And, as she had proven many times before, Nolaa Tarkona was always true to her word. . . .

When the helmeted Boba Fett marched alone into the grotto, Nolaa sat up with a stab of disappointment. Had he *dared* to come back to her empty-handed?

Beside the bounty hunter, claws extended, Hovrak walked like a security escort. But

Boba Fett exuded such self-confidence, even through his Mandalorian armor, that any idea of his *following* anyone was ludicrous. Nolaa admired him for that self-assurance and enigmatic charisma. Fett, however, did not concern himself with power or politics. Why he kept to himself—hiring out only as a bounty hunter, when he could have been a great leader—was a mystery to her. *Ah, well*, she thought, *every creature has different goals*.

"Where is Bornan Thul?" she demanded. "You contracted to bring him back to me, along with the navicomputer I paid for. Why have you returned here without your bounty? Surely you don't intend to report failure?"

"A temporary setback," Fett said, his voice carefully neutral. "I encountered the children of Han Solo; they were unable to provide the information I required. I have other leads." He paused for a moment. "When hunting bounty, I can never be sure what I will find—it is not always what I set out to look for."

More to the point, Nolaa's spies had reported that Jacen and Jaina Solo and their friends had actually foiled Fett out in the Alderaan rubble field, and he had fled in defeat. But she did not mention this. The bounty hunter knew he had failed thus far, and so did she. Nothing else mattered.

"Make no mistake, Boba Fett," Nolaa said, "about the importance of this mission. I must have the cargo Bornan Thul stole. The future of the galaxy depends on it. Until today, I have let only a few other bounty hunters know of my interest—and I suspect some still intend to succeed where you failed. Now, however, you give me no choice but to announce this opportunity to bounty hunters far and wide."

"Send out whomever you like, but *I* shall find Bornan Thul," Fett said. His brusque tone was not threatening, but simply confident. "I am the best. I will succeed. The others will fail."

"Then next time bring me the bounty—not words," Nolaa said.

When Fett turned without bidding her farewell, she raised her clawed hand and called after him to stop. "I have a question—something that intrigues me. I've heard about how Princess Leia Organa once wore a helmet as a disguise, passing herself off as the bounty hunter Boushh to infiltrate Jabba's palace. No one knew her identity until she was caught trying to free Han Solo. Tell me, Boba Fett: under that helmet, and behind your voice synthesizer, are you perhaps . . . a female yourself?"

Fett stared at her through the narrow black slit in his helmet. "I remove my helmet for no one," he said.

But Nolaa would not be distracted. "For that matter," she said, "are you even human? Could you perhaps be one of the downtrodden alien species in this galaxy passing yourself off as a human?"

"I remove my helmet for no one," he repeated, still giving her no answer.

"A pity," Nolaa said. "You may go."

Boba Fett departed with brisk steps, as if incensed that she had given him leave to go when he would never have bothered to ask her permission.

Nolaa sat back in her stone chair, bathed in the bloody red light. It was long past her rest period, but she decided to linger a while yet . . . perhaps much longer. Possibilities for the future continued to develop in her mind.

3

MORNING MIST SETTLED on the grass-stubble clearing in front of the rebuilt Great Temple. Droplets of falling moisture clung to Tenel Ka's warrior braids and sparkled there like a fine spray of gems. Leaning against the damp hull of the *Rock Dragon*, she watched with mixed feelings as Jacen prepared to board the *Shadow Chaser* with Raynar and Master Skywalker.

She knew Jacen would have preferred to fly beside her and she was proud of him for sacrificing his personal preferences to help Raynar, who needed the support of a friend right now. Tenel Ka understood the inner torment of being constantly in danger, constantly on guard. She could have requested to be included on the *Shadow Chaser*, but because the *Rock Dragon* was her ship, Tenel Ka felt duty-bound to remain with her crew—"Captain" Jaina, copilot Lowie, and backup navigator Em Teedee.

Still, Tenel Ka would miss her friend during the trip to the rendezvous point with Raynar's family. She had come to rely on Jacen in an odd sort of way. Somehow, his clowning and joking reassured her that all was well with the galaxy . . . even when all was *not* well. Tenel Ka shook her head to clear it. Allowing her thoughts to dwell on such sentimentalism was unlike her.

Jaina and Lowie chose that moment to emerge from the *Rock Dragon* behind her. Jaina, serious in her duties as captain of the ship, gave an immediate report. "Internal preflight checks are complete—inside's all ready to go. You done with the externals yet?"

Tenel Ka gave a guilty start. She had allowed herself to become distracted! They were heading into a potentially dangerous situation, and she could not afford to let her mind wander. Wiping a sheen of rain from her forehead, she vowed not to let it happen again. "Ten more minutes."

Jaina nodded, then a look of perplexity

stole over her face. She bit her lower lip. "Am I forgetting anything?"

Lowie pointed a ginger-furred arm toward the *Shadow Chaser* and gave a short bark.

"Coordinates. Right," Jaina said. "We have to get the coordinates for our hyperspace jump from Uncle Luke and Raynar. Information came in about an hour ago by tight-beam encrypted transmission. Unregistered proprietary encryption. Raynar was the only one who knew how to decode it."

Tenel Ka was surprised. Such precautions were commonly employed in communications between members of the Hapan royal family, but they were almost unheard of in the New Republic.

While Lowie and Jaina went to consult with Master Skywalker and Raynar, Tenel Ka returned to her preflight check. Chiding herself for her temporary lack of diligence, she examined the rain-slick hull of the *Rock Dragon* as carefully as if she were preparing for a space battle—which, for all she knew, might just be the case.

When Jacen poked his head around the side of the ship to see if she needed any help, Tenel Ka accepted gladly. She didn't actually require assistance, of course, but she welcomed his companionship.

After they'd finished, Jacen said, "I, um . . . I put a little extra sealant on that blast scar Boba Fett gave us in the Alderaan system." He ran a hand through his damp hair. "It looked a bit weak, and I didn't want you to take any chances." Jacen shrugged, perhaps embarrassed at showing his concern for her. "Hey, you can never tell when you're going to bump into another bounty hunter, you know?"

Tenel Ka's cool gray eyes locked onto his. The *Shadow Chaser's* quantum armor would keep its passengers safe if they came under attack. Jacen knew he would be well protected, but he had no similar guarantee for his friends in the *Rock Dragon*. She did her best to reassure him.

"Jacen, my friend, I am used to dealing with traitors, kidnappers, and assassins. The Hapan court is filled with them." One corner of her mouth quirked upward. "In fact, some of the most skilled ones are my relatives. I will not allow the *Rock Dragon* or anyone in her to come to harm."

He nodded, then shrugged again. "I just

like to know everyone's safe. I even made Tionne promise to take care of my gort egg while we're gone." Then, as if chagrined at having been caught worrying, Jacen said, "Hey, wanna hear a joke?"

On the pretext of examining a stabilizer fin Tenel Ka ducked her head to hide her pleasure. If Jacen ever suspected that she actually enjoyed his jokes, he would *really* worry. When she had composed herself again, she looked up and raised an eyebrow at him. "Only if you do not require me to laugh."

"Buzz buzz," he said, then waited expectantly.

After a moment, she realized the response he wanted. "Ah—who is there?"

"Dismay."

"Dismay who?"

"Dismay not seem funny to you, but I'm hoping you'll at least smile."

Tenel Ka nodded judiciously. "Perhaps I will laugh later, my friend Jacen." The absurdity of his humor amazed her. Even more amazing was the fact that the joke had put her at ease again. She closed her eyes, let out a slow breath, and savored the refreshing mist falling from above.

"Hey, you two," Jaina yelled from around the side of the ship, "Coordinates are in. Uncle Luke is locking Artoo down in the astromech station. What are we waiting for?"

Tenel Ka opened her eyes. Jacen gave her hand a brief squeeze. "See you at the rendezvous point," he said.

"This is a fact," Tenel Ka agreed, and Jacen dashed across the damp grass to the *Shadow Chaser*.

For once, compared with the other passenger, Jacen felt more than competent to serve as copilot of a starship. Leaning forward from his seat behind them in the cockpit, Raynar hovered anxiously between Jacen and Master Skywalker, eyeing the control panels as if to ensure that Jacen wouldn't make a mistake.

Jacen tried to calm the young man. He even sent subtle, soothing thoughts, as he might to a frightened animal. But once they left Yavin 4, Raynar's agitation increased minute by minute. By the time the *Shadow Chaser* made its jump to hyperspace, Jacen felt edgy himself.

Even the normally patient Master Skywalker turned with a strained smile and said, "I can take it from here, Jacen. Why don't you two go in the back and practice a few Jedi relaxation exercises? I'll call you when we're ready to make our rendezvous with the fleet."

"I'm not sure I *can* relax," Raynar said. But when Jacen unbuckled his crash webbing and headed back toward the crew compartment, the other young man obediently followed.

Before Jacen could leave the cockpit, however, Raynar turned back. "Master Skywalker, are you *sure* you have the coordinates right?"

"I programmed them in myself from your notes when you decoded the transmission," Luke said, and when Raynar seemed about to ask for more details, he added, "Jaina and Lowbacca confirmed coordinates for both the *Shadow Chaser* and the *Rock Dragon*. We're fine."

The answer appeared to satisfy Raynar, who finally let Jacen lead him into the back. Jacen took a deep breath, held it for a few heartbeats, and slowly released it. Then, to break the tension, he said, "I guess you're pretty scared."

Raynar sat down, shoulders hunched over, and stared at the deckplates. "How would *you* feel if somebody in your family was missing and maybe even dead?"

From the astromech station, Artoo-Detoo whistled a mournful note.

Jacen gave a humorless laugh. "Believe it or not, that situation isn't completely uncommon in my family. I know how you feel."

Raynar looked up at Jacen. A smile tugged at the corner of his mouth. "Yeah, I guess you do at that."

An hour later when Luke called them back to the cockpit, both boys were more relaxed. Raynar even attempted a joke or two. Jacen already knew the punch lines, but he laughed anyway because it was so funny to hear the normally pompous boy working so hard to use humor. The kid wasn't too bad, Jacen decided, but he needed a little work on his timing and delivery.

As soon as they buckled themselves into their seats, Raynar began to show signs of nervousness again. "Why don't you tell Uncle Luke your joke, Raynar?" Jacen said.

"The one about the nerf herder and the purple rancor?"

"Maybe later," Luke said. "We're just about there. Okay . . . now," he said, nodding to Jacen.

Jacen leaned forward and disengaged the hyperdrive. The starlines shortened abruptly and resolved themselves into a million twinkling lights in the blackness of space.

Empty space, without any merchant ships anywhere in sight.

Jacen blinked in surprise. "Where are they?" He asked. "What happened to the fleet?"

Luke Skywalker looked at the control panel, perplexed. "These are the coordinates they gave me."

"They're gone," Raynar said in a gloomy voice. "The fleet has left without me."

Jacen adjusted the volume controls as the cockpit speaker crackled to life. "*Shadow Chaser*, this is *Rock Dragon*," Jaina's voice said. "Kinda lonely out here. Weren't we expecting company?"

"Still waiting to make contact," Jacen answered. "Uncle Luke says—"

From the comm speaker a new female voice cut through his transmission. "*Shadow Chaser* and *Rock Dragon*, please broadcast confirmation of your identities."

At Luke's nod, Jacen complied. They waited. "Identities confirmed," the voice said at last. "This is the *Tryst*. I am prepared to take you—"

"Where is my mother? Where is the fleet?" Raynar cut in. "They were supposed to meet us here. What have you done with them?"

"Ah, would that be Master Raynar Thul?" the voice answered. "This is your second cousin, Captain Dro Prack, of the security shuttle *Tryst* assigned to the *Tradewyn*. Now if you'll all be so kind as to slave your navigational computers to mine, we can be on our way to rendezvous with the fleet."

"Um, shuttle *Tryst*?" Jaina's voice came over the speaker. "We were under the impression that this *was* the rendezvous point."

"That was the impression we intended you to have," Captain Prack said. "This was just an intermediate stop to make sure no one followed you."

"What if it's a trap? I've barely met most

of my second cousins," Raynar said in a low voice. "We, uh, have a large extended family. Half of them left Alderaan decades ago when the Emperor came into power." In spite of the relaxation exercises he'd been doing, Raynar looked agitated again.

"Can you confirm that she really works for your family?" Luke asked.

"Is there a question you can ask her?" Jacen added. "Maybe some kind of secret code your family uses in emergencies?"

Raynar thought for a moment, then said in a loud voice, "Captain Prack, which of our great family treasures was saved by a fortunate coincidence when the Death Star blew up Alderaan?"

"Simple enough," Prack answered, her voice casual and confident. "The Dro ceremonial fountain had been sent to Calamari to be repaired by the renowned artist Myrrack. Therefore the Dro family's great treasure was safely off-planet and spared from destruction."

Raynar's ruddy face beamed. "That's it. No one but a member of my family would know the answer to that question."

"You're sure?" Luke asked.

Raynar nodded. "Trust me."

"Raynar says you passed the test," Jacen said into the comm speaker. "We're slaving the *Shadow Chaser*'s navigational computers to yours."

"*Rock Dragon* slaving over to *Tryst*," Jaina's voice said.

"All right, everybody," Captain Prack answered, "hold on to your seats."

Starlines swooped and stuttered around the *Shadow Chaser* as the *Tryst* took them on three consecutive jumps through hyperspace, none more than a minute long. Then, suddenly, they were there.

A ragtag assortment of merchant vessels, security shuttles, cargo ships, star skimmers, and scout cruisers drifted before them in space. The fleet held ships of all sizes and manufactures, designed for versatile operations in different shipping environments. Over the years, Bornan and Aryn Thul had expanded their merchant operation into a massive undertaking. But now, out of concern for their safety, the Thul family could not allow their fleet a permanent base.

"This is it," Raynar said. "My real home."

4

RAYNAR FILLED HIS lungs with the cool, recycled air on the *Tradewyn*, flagship of his family's merchant fleet. His father had always insisted that the *Tradewyn* have the finest filters and recyclers available. For business reasons, the fleet's headquarters remained on Coruscant, but this vessel—more than any other place in the galaxy—had become the family's home.

His mother claimed that the air on Alderaan had been sweeter, though by the time of Raynar's birth that planet had already been space rubble for years. He had been born here, on the *Tradewyn* itself. For him, no place could feel safer or more welcoming in a time of danger.

Raynar closed his eyes, taking a second deep breath, and a third. For so long he had smelled the humidity and the lush, thick jungle scents of Yavin 4. This seemed so much purer.

Behind him, he heard Luke and the young Jedi Knights climb out of the *Shadow Chaser* and the *Rock Dragon*, then thump to the deckplates, but he did not allow that to distract him from his enjoyment. He had so many memories of this place.

To Raynar's embarrassment, he was dangerously close to tears when he heard the docking-bay airlock *whoosh* open. He felt a comforting hand on his shoulder, and Master Skywalker said in a low voice, "It's always good to feel that you've come home. Are you all right, Raynar?"

Dismayed that Master Skywalker had sensed this weakness in him, Raynar's first impulse was to draw himself up and make some sort of haughty reply to indicate that he was fully in control of himself. But instead, he took another deep breath—this time a calming one, as part of a Jedi relaxation technique—opened his eyes, and nodded. A true Jedi had little need to lie, or even pretend. In this case, he knew the only one he could fool would be himself.

"Thank you. I'll be fine now," Raynar

said. Glancing at the airlock, he saw his mother, Aryn Dro Thul, hurrying toward him, accompanied by his uncle Tyko.

Tyko Thul wore the voluminous yellow, purple, orange, and scarlet robes of the family house. His moon-round face beamed as brightly as an emergency glow beacon. "My dear boy, how comforting it is to see you safely arrived! Here with us, you have nothing to fear."

Raynar's surprise at seeing his uncle again was compounded by his mother's next action. She stepped forward and awkwardly—for their family had never been physically demonstrative—gave Raynar a hug. Recovering quickly from his shock, he hugged her back, then stepped away and cleared his throat. "M-m-mother, Uncle Tyko, I have some friends I'd like you to meet. This is Master Skywalker of the Jedi academy."

His mother stretched out both of her hands to clasp Luke's in a traditional greeting. "Luke Skywalker, hero of the Rebellion," she said with a warm smile, "it's good to see you again. And how kind of you to bring my son to me."

"I promised my sister Leia that I would

see you personally, Aryn Dro Thul, and make sure that you're all safe here," he replied.

"Please thank Chief of State Leia Organa Solo for us," Aryn said, obviously touched.

Next, Tyko reached his hands out to grip Luke's. "Master Skywalker, it is an honor. Alas, it would have been an even greater honor to meet you on Mechis III, so that I could extend my personal hospitality at the droid works there. I think you would be most impressed."

Master Skywalker's smile looked as if he were trying to repress some secret amusement. "Thank you. I've heard a great deal about your successes on Mechis III. Your droid works are the most . . . productive in the New Republic."

Uncle Tyko beamed even more brightly than before. "It's nothing really," he said, with a vain attempt at a modest shrug. "Success seems to come naturally to my family. To me, to my brother—I daresay you've noticed it even in Raynar. I'm certain he quite surpasses most of your other students in sheer Jedi ability."

Raynar felt his cheeks warm with discomfiture. How could Master Skywalker respond to such a display of pompous self-importance?

To his credit, however, the Jedi Master answered smoothly and without hesitation. "Raynar is a unique and earnest student who has more Jedi potential than even he is aware of."

Before his uncle could push Master Skywalker further, Raynar broke in. "And I'd like you to meet some of my fellow students: Jaina and Jacen Solo, Lowbacca from Kashyyyk, and Tenel Ka, a princess of Hapes and Dathomir."

Uncle Tyko pursed his lips in surprise. "Very distinguished guests," he observed.

"They certainly are," Raynar's mother said. "You are all welcome to stay as long as you like. I think this calls for a celebration." Her midnight-blue gown, shot with silver thread and belted with a sash in the colors of the House of Thul, glittered like the star-studded wedges of space visible through the viewports.

"I'm afraid I must return to the Jedi academy as soon as possible," Master Skywalker said with a regretful shake of his head. "Artoo and I need to get back. We have many other students and much work to do."

"But *we'd* like to stay," Jacen hurried to assure Aryn Dro Thul. "Just for a few days, of course, to make sure that Raynar's okay and settling in here."

Lowie urffed his support of the plan.

"Why, what a splendid idea!" Em Teedee said. "Civilization, at last."

The details and arrangements were soon settled. Jacen, Jaina, Lowie and Tenel Ka would stay for five days, then return to the Jedi academy in the *Rock Dragon*.

In less than half an hour, Luke Skywalker and Artoo-Detoo departed in the *Shadow Chaser*. Raynar's mother sighed as she watched their sleek ship vanish. "Well, I suppose we'll have to make another hyperspace jump now, just to keep moving."

Uncle Tyko nodded. "To be sure no one can follow us by picking up on the *Shadow Chaser*'s log of recent stops."

Raynar's mother clasped her hands and smiled. "When that's done, I have a special treat for you children. To celebrate my son's return, you're all invited to an Alderaanian Ceremony of Waters!"

• • •

The Ceremony of Waters was long and elaborate, and apparently filled with great meaning for the Thul family . . . but Jacen found his mind wandering during the endless rituals. He squirmed and tried to sit up straighter on the hard narrow bench that ringed the small, elegant fountain that served as a centerpiece for the ceremony.

He absently reached to where his lightsaber usually hung at his side, planning to run his fingers along its ridges, as he often did when he was bored . . . but then he remembered the weapon wasn't there. Everyone had been asked to change into their best clothes for this special occasion. And since it was a ritual of peace, all the young Jedi had left their weapons in their cabins.

Aryn Thul, her long chestnut hair braided in an intricate pattern, looked beautiful and serene in her midnight-blue gown. The hairstyle reminded Jacen of his mother. Sometimes he wondered how Leia managed to put up with all the boring ceremonies, rituals, and meetings her duties as Chief of State required her to endure. In times past, Jacen, Jaina, and their younger brother Anakin had often attended events their mother thought they might especially enjoy. Even at those, however, Jacen had frequently found himself wishing he were out with his friend Zekk exploring the fascinating, and sometimes dangerous, lower levels of Coruscant.

Jacen remembered a disastrous time when he and Jaina had persuaded Zekk to be their guest at a simple state dinner. Had that experience been this bewildering—this *excruciating*—for the dark-haired young man? He missed Zekk. Letting his eyes drift around the room, Jacen wondered if anyone else was as bored as he was.

On the other side of the fountain, Raynar and Tyko sat flanking Aryn Thul while she performed the ceremony. All three were apparently engrossed in every detail of the rituals. Beside him, Jaina watched attentively as Aryn filled an array of brightly colored transparent flasks, cups, and beakers. At Jacen's left, Tenel Ka sat laser-straight, her cool gray eyes dutifully following each step. Completing the circle, his eyes half closed, Jacen noticed Lowie taking this opportunity to practice his Jedi relaxation techniques . . . or perhaps just napping. Em Teedee's glowing optical sensors were alert, though the little droid made no sound.

Setting aside the last of the filled vessels, Aryn Thul began to hum a slow, lilting tune. As she did so, she held her hands under one of the clear streams of liquid that gurgled from the fountain. Water flowed across the backs of her hands, and then she turned them over, letting the water run into her palms. Still humming, she nodded. Raynar and Tyko placed their hands under the trickling water as well.

Tenel Ka—always fast to catch on—stretched her arm out and held her hand under the stream of water. Jacen noticed the glow of pleasure that lit Aryn's and Raynar's eyes at this. Lowie opened his eyes at the same time that Jaina nudged Jacen. Six more hands entered the flow from the fountain. Jacen was amazed to find the water warm and silky to the touch.

The remainder of the ceremony consisted of drying their hands, then passing around the various cups and beakers. Aryn hummed while Tyko or Raynar recited words about purity or peace or the life-giving qualities of water. Then they would sip from the beaker or empty it and refill it from the fountain or sprinkle drops in the air to fall like rain. Occasionally, Em Tedee even hummed along with Aryn; Raynar's mother did not seem to mind.

Jacen was glad, at least, to see Raynar distracted from his misery. The blond-haired boy looked happier than Jacen had ever seen him on Yavin 4.

When the humming stopped, Raynar's uncle Tyko let out a long sigh. "It's wonderful to be among civilized beings again," he said. "You have no idea what it's like to live and work on Mechis III, surrounded all day long by mechanicals. We keep only a few living beings on the planet, and very few of *them* come from worlds with culture. Of course, I've programmed a droid or two for protocol, but it's simply not the same. They're so dull."

"Well, really!" Em Teedee exclaimed before Lowie slapped a furry hand over the translating droid's speaker grille.

"This is my favorite ceremony," Raynar said wistfully.

"Mine too," his mother agreed. "It reminds me of the days when I lived on Alderaan. I grew up in Terrarium City," she said. "My parents were on the ruling council. It was a beautiful serene place, and every home was surrounded by plants and fountains like this one. I left to study at Alderaan University."

"Where you met father," Raynar put in.

"Yes." Her forehead wrinkled slightly at the mention of her kidnapped husband. "I was studying music and business, and Bornan was studying business and art. We took several courses together and found we had similar goals. When we finished our studies, we formed this trading company."

"Where were you when Alderaan was destroyed?" Jaina asked in a hushed voice.

Aryn flinched, struck by yet another painful memory. "Sometimes I wish I'd never left, that I could have spent those last few days there. . . ." She sighed. "Bornan is an excellent businessman, and he believes in overseeing negotiations personally. We were in the middle of very sensitive trade talks with one of the Imperial worlds when our home was obliterated."

Aryn seemed lost in her reverie when a guard entered the room, bent down, and whispered in her ear.

"What is it, Mother?" Raynar asked.

Aryn scanned the circle with a look of alarm. Then she turned to the security officer. "It's all right. Tell them," she said.

"A few minutes ago security noted a brief transmission that came from inside the *Tradewyn*. We tried to trace it, but couldn't find the source."

Raynar clasped his mother's hand. Uncle Tyko stood abruptly. "Prepare for another hyperspace jump," he said to the guard. "Immediately!"

The guard rushed to carry out his orders. Tyko looked down at his sister-in-law. "It can't be anyone here in this room," he said, "but I fear we may have a traitor aboard the *Tradewyn*."

5

FOR JAINA, THE bridge of the *Tradewyn* was a wonderland filled with the highest quality computers, gadgets, and communications equipment available in any market. She and Lowie exclaimed over each discovery of technological wizardry.

She thought briefly of her friend Zekk, with whom she had spent many of her younger days on Coruscant, scavenging technological gadgets from the abandoned underlevels and tinkering with them so that old Peckhum could have something to sell. She and Zekk had gone their separate ways, though. He had fallen to the dark side and joined the Shadow Academy.

Even after he had been defeated, and forgiven, Zekk still could not forgive himself. He had struck out on his own in hopes of building a new life. He had decided to become a bounty hunter, and Jaina wished she could contact him somehow, and get news of him in return. But here, hidden as they were with the Bornaryn merchant fleet, no one in the galaxy would know where to find them.

After the Ceremony of Waters, Raynar took turns with his mother conducting the tour of the flagship, and proved almost as knowledgeable as she was on the subject.

The young Jedi had come to the bridge while Tyko prepared the ship for its next hyperspace jump, hoping to keep one step ahead of any pursuers that might be after them or Bornan Thul. The *Tradewyn*'s jump elicited a tingle of excitement from the Jedi students. All of them had seen many such jumps, but rarely from the open bridge of a city-sized starship. Tyko paced the bridge, a heavy frown corrugating his forehead, his hands clasped behind his back, as Raynar and Aryn Dro Thul continued the tour.

"What are those?" Jaina asked, spying an unusual console.

"Our weapons systems," Aryn replied.

"Targeting for the entire fleet is linked through here."

"Everything can be controlled from the bridge of the *Tradewyn*," Raynar added. "Concussion missiles, ion cannons, even targeted energy deflectors. We have quad laser emplacements all around the circumference of the bridge—there, there, and there—" he said, pointing, "plus one up top and one below us. Of course, we can also release control to individual gunners."

Jaina eyed the weapons appraisingly. "I'd love to try them sometime. Dad always lets us practice with the guns in the *Millennium Falcon*."

Aryn's eyebrows went up. "Ah, yes, that doesn't surprise me. Your father always was a bit of a rogue. I met him briefly, on Alderaan, when—"

"You know Han Solo?" Raynar broke in, his eyes wide.

Aryn laughed. "Not really. It was decades ago, before I was married, and he visited Alderaan for a day. Of course, he was traveling under another name at the time. We just happened to meet. Back then, I thought he was very handsome. He even tried to steal me from your father. Bornan was rather jealous." Aryn's fine-boned face dimpled in a warm smile. "Even though Han has been a respectable man for many years, I'm afraid Bornan may still harbor a bit of a grudge."

"Preparing to come out of hyperspace," the helmsman announced in a loud voice.

"Very well," Tyko said. "You, over there." He pointed to a man in a security uniform near the navigational station. "Begin plotting our next jump, just to be on the safe side."

"Kusk," the man replied. "We've been introduced several times."

Tyko blinked. "I beg your pardon?"

"Kusk, sir—it's my name."

Uncle Tyko made a face as if he had bitten into a chunk of rancid nerf cheese. "Very well—*Kusk*. I suggest you begin plotting our course immediately or we'll stuff you into an escape pod and shoot you toward the nearest inhabited system. Do I make myself clear?"

"Yes, sir," Kusk gritted between clenched teeth.

Jaina made a mental note never to cross Raynar's uncle Tyko. She wouldn't want to be on the receiving end of his anger.

Just then the scene in the viewports all around the bridge changed. Starlines shortened from glowing streaks into specks of concentrated brilliance, and they were alone against the blackness of space. Completely alone. Not a single ship from the fleet had made the jump with the *Tradewyn*.

No. Not alone. Something else *was* here . . . waiting for them, ready to pounce.

Lowie saw it first and sounded the alarm. "Oh, my! We're doomed," Em Teedee wailed.

There in the viewscreen closest to them came a wicked-looking ship that was no part of their fleet. Its weapons were powered up, ready to fire.

Jacen wished he could think of something to do.

"We're receiving a transmission, Lady Aryn," the communications specialist said. "Priority one."

"Put it on the front viewscreen," Tyko snapped.

The comm specialist looked back at Aryn. She nodded.

A face masked by a dark flight helmet appeared on screen. "*Tradewyn*, this is the

High Roller," the harsh voice came over the comm speakers. "I demand that you release to me either Aryn Dro Thul or Raynar Thul immediately. If you refuse, I will be forced to destroy your ship."

Although this seemed like an absurd demand to Jacen, he was still surprised when Uncle Tyko gave a bark of laughter. "This ship has the finest defenses and weaponry that can be bought. Don't force us to prove it."

On the screen, the helmeted figure shrugged. "Perhaps you have the best defenses that can be bought—*legally*, that is—but I have access to sources you couldn't even begin to imagine." An energy bolt streaked out from the ship and struck just below the forward viewport. "If you give me the woman or the boy," the harsh voice said, "I won't need to demonstrate any further. You have ten minutes to decide."

"Screen off," Tyko snapped. The viewscreen went blank. "We need to clear the bridge of everyone but essential bridge crew. Kusk, take Lady Aryn down to the security shelter at the center of the ship. Don't let anyone near her until this threat has been dealt with. Get moving! Raynar, you go too."

Kusk sprang up from the navigational console with commendable speed, now that he had been chided by Tyko, and hustled Raynar and his mother from the bridge before Tyko could issue the next order. Even Aryn did not argue. As they vanished down the turbolift, Raynar looked worriedly back over his shoulder, although he tried to appear brave in front of his friends.

Jacen was glad the security guard had reacted quickly this time and avoided making a scene. Even so, he got a strange prickly feeling at the back of his neck. He shivered. Something was wrong here. . . .

Maybe it was because the *High Roller* was outside the viewports waiting to blast the bridge again, but he didn't think so. Beside him, Tenel Ka stood up straighter and glanced around as if searching for something. Their eyes met. She felt it too.

"Now," Tyko said, "I'll need the rest of you children off the bridge. We're going to be in the middle of a firefight. All weapons, power up and calibrate your targeting systems!"

Jaina stepped forward boldly. "I could be

some help to you here. I have a lot of gunnery experience." She looked over at Jacen. "I'm a pretty good shot and so is—"

Jacen, feeling an urgent need to follow Raynar, gave a minute shake of his head.

"—uh, so is Lowie," Jaina went on, catching the hint, though she didn't seem to understand her brother's intentions.

Lowie cocked his head in surprise, then smoothed the fur down on his neck with both hands. He gave a sharp bark of agreement.

"Very well, then. You may both stay. We'll need all the help we can get," Uncle Tyko said. "But the rest of you, to your quarters until the emergency has passed."

Jacen and Tenel Ka hurried from the bridge and into the turbolift. When the door slid shut behind them, Tenel Ka raised her eyebrows. "Are you thinking the same as I?"

Jacen nodded. "I'm thinking that Aryn and Raynar may not be safe even down in the protected chambers. Something is very wrong here."

Tenel Ka made a fist and thumped it against her bare thigh. "This is a fact."

• • •

"He's somewhere on this level," Jacen said, stepping out of the turbolift. "I can sense him."

"But we are nowhere close to the center of the ship," Tenel Ka pointed out. "I believe we have reached the docking bays. The guard should not have brought Aryn and Raynar here."

Jacen swallowed hard. "Yeah, that's what I was afraid of," he said. "I've got a bad feeling about this."

As if to prove his intuition correct, a blaster shot rang out from down the corridor. "Hey, that came from the docking bay down there!" Jacen said. "Isn't that where—"

Tenel Ka's face was grim. "Yes. Where we left the *Rock Dragon*."

Suddenly, the flagship thrummed with a sharp impact, as if someone had struck the hull with a giant hammer—or a powerful turbolaser blast. "I think that deadline the *High Roller* gave us just expired," Jacen said.

They ran.

The *Tradewyn* hummed as it fired back

at the ship that had ambushed it. The space battle had begun.

When they reached the entrance to the docking bay, a strange sight greeted them. His face flushed, Raynar stood protectively in front of his mother near the boarding ramp to the *Rock Dragon*, colorful robes swirling around him like an aurora.

Closer to the entrance, the guard Kusk faced them, speaking into a comlink gripped in one hand. His other hand held a blaster aimed more or less at Raynar. The blaster, however, seemed to have a mind of its own. It raised and lowered and wobbled and dipped while Kusk wrestled to hold it steady. Obviously, Raynar was struggling through the Force to get a grip on Kusk's weapon.

"Yes, I have the merchandise you requested," Kusk said into the comlink, straining to keep hold of his squirming weapon. "I'll meet you in five minutes at the pickup point."

A harsh voice replied. Though it was crackly with static, Jacen still recognized it as the voice of the helmeted man aboard the *High Roller*. "It worked, just like I said it would."

Another blow struck the ship. The mysterious attacker had shot again, but the guard Kusk merely smiled in satisfaction. The *Tradewyn* fired back with a loud whining discharge of deadly energy.

Tenel Ka took her own action. "Prepare to fight, traitor!" she said in a loud voice. She stepped forward, ready for battle.

"Hey—I have a feeling your plans aren't going to turn out quite as well as you thought, Kusk," Jacen said. He wished fleetingly that he and Tenel Ka were wearing their lightsabers, but they had removed them for the Ceremony of Waters.

Sliding his comlink through a loop in his belt, Kusk faced the door, only mildly surprised by the intruders. His lip curled in a sneer. "I don't really think three children and a woman can do much to thwart the plans of a trained killer and a seasoned bounty hunter." He turned back toward his quarry. Aryn Thul glared contemptuously at the traitorous guard.

Raynar squared his shoulders. "Maybe not," he said. "But there's a great deal that three *Jedi* can do."

As the guard snorted in disdain, another hammer blow from the attacker struck the

Tradewyn. Taking advantage of the distraction, Jacen administered a hard Force shove against the guard's back. At the same moment Tenel Ka lifted Kusk a few centimeters off the floor with her mind, throwing him off balance. Raynar held out one arm, and the astonished guard's blaster finally spun from his grasp into the young man's outstretched hand.

"Don't hurt him," Aryn cautioned in a loud voice. "We'll need him alive to learn how far this conspiracy goes."

Kusk's feet thumped down onto the deckplates. Open-mouthed, he retreated as if pulled by invisible strings until his back pressed against the hull of the *Rock Dragon*. His eyes darted in panic from Jacen and Tenel Ka to Raynar and Aryn and back again.

"How did you do that?" he rasped.

Jacen crossed his arms over his chest. "We're Jedi. One of my best friends is training to be a bounty hunter," he said, thinking of Zekk. "And you violated one of their most fundamental rules: Always do your research."

Kusk snatched at his comlink. "*High*

Roller, this is Kusk. I've been captured.
Save yourself."

Aryn strode to the comm panel by the
airlock door. "Security backup team to
secondary docking bay—immediately," she
said in a calm, commanding voice. Red
lights strobed and sirens whooped. Kusk
flailed for the entry hatch of the *Rock
Dragon* and attempted to pull himself inside.

"I wouldn't, if I were you," Tenel Ka said.
Kusk hesitated for just a moment. "My
ship has a fail-safe navigational program,"
she explained. "Unless my crew or I input
the proper authorization code, the ship is
programmed to find the most direct route
to Hapes and dock at the high-security
hangar of the Hapan royal house." She
smiled coldly. "Not even you would want to
explain yourself to my parents, my grand-
mother, and the seven hundred hand-picked
guards stationed there."

A burst of static blasted from the comlink in Kusk's hand. He dropped it as if it
were a venomous reptile and sank to the
floor. The next moment the *Tradewyn*'s
security squad arrived. One of the guards
stopped to report. "That particular bounty

hunter won't be bothering you anymore," she said to Aryn Thul. "We sustained only minimal damage, but the *High Roller* made an unlucky bet. The ship is completely destroyed. No survivors."

"Thank you," Raynar's mother said.

A thin wail rose from the floor next to the *Rock Dragon*. Jacen could just barely make out the words of Kusk's mournful cry: "My brother!"

6

STILL TRYING TO make peace with the memories of his Dark Jedi days, Zekk eagerly sought out an assignment to begin his new career as a bounty hunter. As a first step toward finding an employer, he went to the most bustling place he could think of—a bazaar of traders and smugglers, scam artists, lawbreakers, and opportunists, inside the hollow center of asteroid Borgo Prime. From there, he hoped to establish his credentials, while adhering to the Bounty Hunters Creed.

At a loss after his arrival, he spent days wandering through the airlocked, low-gravity city. He moved from establishment to establishment, putting out the word that he was looking for work as a bounty hunter. He also made numerous inquiries about the most recent known location of a man named Bornan Thul. It seemed every bounty hunter in the galaxy had set out to find Thul, and if Zekk could succeed, his name would become famous indeed.

Many people laughed at his youthful optimism and his battered ship. Zekk fought hard to keep his anger in check, but when his emerald eyes flashed, most of those who had joked at his expense fell silent and turned away. Naturally, Zekk could tap into the Force if he wanted to, but it frightened him to do so. He dreaded the possibility of slipping again into the endless gulf of the dark side, a place from which he knew he would never escape a second time.

One afternoon, he found his way into a popular interspecies bar called Shanko's Hive, whose insectoid caretaker was famous for using his many arms and legs to whirl about, mixing several drinks at the same time. Shanko hibernated for a month out of every year, though, and when Zekk entered the hive he found that the insect had cocooned himself in his chambers and would not return again for some time.

Shanko had left management of the bar

in the capable hands—the capable *three* hands, actually—of his lead bartender, Droq'l. The three-armed, blue-skinned semi-humanoid had two eyes centered in the middle of his head, another in the back, and one on top of his bald blue skull.

"Bornan Thul, eh?" the bartender said, washing glasses with one hand and mixing a drink with another, while the third arm (which protruded from the center of his chest) reached forward to shake Zekk's hand. "You do know that Nolaa Tarkona has put out a widespread call, now don't you? She's offering enough credits to interest every bounty hunter in the galaxy."

"Yes. And you do know that most of them aren't as good as I am, now don't you?" Zekk countered.

"I see you don't lack in self-confidence," Droq'l answered with a smile, flashing glossy black teeth.

"No," Zekk answered. "No I don't."

At one table in the back of the bar two squealing Ranats threw glowing dice at each other and attempted to catch them in their long, ratlike snouts. It appeared to be some sort of a game rather than an argument.

Suddenly loud sirens erupted, along with clanging, whoops, flashing lights, and ringing bells. Zekk jumped to attention, fully alert and ready to defend himself. "What is it? What happened? Is that an alarm?"

The ear-splitting noise continued without interruption for a full minute. "No, that's just music," Droq'l shouted over the din. "It's that blasted Ishi Tib popular stuff. Most of the other patrons can't stand it,.but—hey—whichever customer puts a credit chip into the music machine gets to pick the tune."

Finally the commotion ended, and the three-armed bartender set another freshly washed glass aside. Leaning across the bar, he placed all three blue elbows on the polished countertop and stared at Zekk with his front pair of eyes. "Listen, kid—I might be able to give you a little errand to run. That is, if you're interested," he said.

"Of course. I'm ready to take on any assignment," Zekk said, a little too enthusiastically.

"Good. I need you to find somebody who said he had a buyer for a small shipment of mine: ronik shells with a premium luster finish. He's a scavenger and a trader, sometimes even a bounty hunter . . . but not too successful at any of those careers. He took off. Haven't heard a thing from him since."

"Who is it?" Zekk said.

Droq'l flipped out a small holo image and switched it on, showing a rodentlike creature with big eyes, large round ears, and a pointed snout. Zekk didn't recognize the species.

"Name's Fonterrat. Not overly trustworthy, but I didn't think he'd have the nerve to skip out on me. I'll pay you a modest bounty if you can find him for me so I can sell that shipment of shells myself." The bartender stared at Zekk intently. "Since you're new at this, you can't command a high fee, of course."

"Of course. I'm out to establish my reputation, and you're providing me with an opportunity—the start I was looking for," Zekk said. "Where do I find this Fonterrat?"

The bartender laughed and clapped all three hands together to mimic a round of applause. "If I knew for certain where to find him, I wouldn't need to hire somebody, now would I?"

"All right," Zekk countered, "where should I *start* to look for him?"

"Now that's a better question," the bartender said. "I knew a bit of Fonterrat's schedule. He had a few other stops—to pick up routing cargo and meet with certain associates . . . but his last scheduled destination was a human colony known as Gammalin. He never came back, and I never received any word from him."

"Gammalin," Zekk said, letting the word burn itself into his memory. "My ship has navigational files, so I'm sure I can find out where that is."

"Good. And when you do find him, you might want to backtrack his route, because . . ."—Droq'l paused for effect, his round eyes twinkling as if he were a child with a secret—"one of those associates Fonterrat was supposed to meet along the way was none other than the person you're trying to find for Nolaa Tarkona's big bounty: Bornan Thul. So, if you do a good job for me, you may just find more than you actually thought you would."

Zekk felt a surge of excitement. "It's a good start, at least! Thanks for the lead. You can count on me."

"Yes, but don't get too cocky. Everyone else in the galaxy is looking for Bornan Thul too, remember?"

"I'll remember. But it doesn't matter," Zekk said. "I don't mind the competition—as long as I'm the one who finds him first."

And with a cheerful wave, he turned and raced back to the *Lightning Rod*.

7

AFTER THE BATTLE against the predatory ship *High Roller*, Lowie climbed out of the quad laser emplacement on the bridge of the *Tradewyn*. Though full of energy and pumped up from the fight, he was also disturbed that the ill-conceived ambush had cost their ruthless attacker his life.

Turning in a slow circle, Lowbacca scanned the viewports, observing the space debris and mangled bits of hull plating that drifted there—all that remained of the bounty hunter's ship. They were safe now . . . at least until the next unexpected attack from someone else with a grudge against the Thul family.

When the weapons officer had been unable to score a hit on the swift *High Roller* from the control console, Tyko had called on Lowie and Jaina to assist him. The attacker's ship had fired relentlessly at the bridge, darting and dodging all return fire— until Lowie and Jaina had joined the fray, with their Jedi-enhanced abilities.

In the end, one of Jaina's shots had taken out the *High Roller*, and the danger from outside was truly over. *For the moment.* Lowie's battle-ready reflexes began to relax, but waves of tension still rolled from the quad laser emplacement where Jaina sat.

A security guard entered the bridge deck, his face grim. He informed Tyko that Officer Kusk had been apprehended while trying to abduct Raynar and Aryn and that Jacen, Tenel Ka, and Raynar himself had thwarted the plan devised by Kusk and his bounty hunter brother. Tyko thrust out his generous lower lip and commented, "Brother? So Kusk was *in* on it. You see, you just can't get good help these days."

Lowie helped a shaky Jaina climb from the quad laser well. Her face remained flushed from the excitement of the space battle, but her brandy-brown eyes were somber. "If Zekk still wants to become a bounty hunter, I hope he never does anything that stupid," she said in a low voice.

Lowie crooned a soft note of understanding.

Tyko Thul approached them, his hands clasped behind his back. "Those bounty hunters must be after all members of the Thul family, including me! Presumably, we can be used as bait to lure Bornan out of hiding." He shook his head. "I wish my brother wasn't so self-centered and foolish. I'm getting a good picture now of what happened," he said. "The *High Roller* must have intended to create a diversion while Kusk kidnapped Aryn and Raynar, then launched them from this ship in an escape pod or any other craft that happened to be available."

"Like the *Rock Dragon*," Jaina said.

Lowie mulled this over, then rumbled his understanding. "Indeed," Em Teedee piped up. "A relatively simple plan."

"So the *High Roller* would have broken off its attack, picked up Kusk and the hostages, then made a quick hop into hyperspace," Jaina said as full comprehension dawned on her.

"But what happened to the rest of the merchant fleet then?" Tyko asked.

Em Teedee made a sound as if he were clearing his throat. "Ahem. If you would allow me, sir, I'd like to access the *Tradewyn*'s computers. I believe I might be able to rectify the situation."

"Direct access to the *Tradewyn*'s computers?" Tyko's eyes narrowed with suspicion. "I've had quite a bit of experience with droids, and I know how susceptible they are to programming glitches. How can I be sure this droid is trustworthy?"

"Programming glitches? Indeed!" Em Teedee huffed at the same moment Lowie let out a roar of offended pride.

Tyko backed away, holding up his hands in a placating gesture. "Very well, very well, be my guest. Just don't tell Aryn I gave you access." In a matter of minutes the Wookiee and Jaina had Em Teedee hooked up to the flagship's bridge computer system.

As he scanned, Em Teedee began making cryptic comments. "Ah, yes. . . . I see. . . . Oh, indeed. . . . Fascinating!"

Jaina listened, biting her lower lip. Finally she could wait no longer. "Mind sharing your insights with us, Em Teedee?"

"Why of course, Mistress Jaina," the little droid said. "How remiss of me. It's just that this machine is so marvelously intelligent, and I—"

Lowie gave an impatient bark.

"Cut to the chase," Jaina said.

"Go on, droid—tell us what happened," Tyko added imperiously.

"Well," Em Teedee began in a defensive voice, "I should think it is intuitively obvious by now. Officer Kusk had the navigational link to all of the fleet's computers. He sent the rest of them false jump coordinates."

"So," Tyko said, "that transmission burst security picked up a few minutes before our last hyperspace jump must have been Kusk sending the true coordinates to his brother the bounty hunter."

"That seems highly likely, sir," Em Teedee agreed. Lowie was interested to see Tyko's attitude change subtly at this indirect praise from the miniaturized translating droid.

"A simple and elegant plan," Tyko said. "Excellent work, droid. Can you plot us a route to where the rest of the fleet is now?"

"Of course, sir. Nothing simpler," Em Teedee said. "I have become quite adept at establishing rapport with starship navicomputers."

Uncle Tyko gave a decisive nod. "Very well, do that." He paused for a moment. "Oh, and, er . . . Em Teedee, is it? When you've finished, can you work out an algorithm for randomizing our hyperspace jumps so that no one will be able to broadcast our coordinates ahead of time?"

"It would be my greatest pleasure, sir," Em Teedee replied with pride.

Apparently satisfied, Tyko retreated to consult with the ship's security staff while other crew members went to call Aryn Dro Thul back to the bridge. Lowie gave Em Teedee a congratulatory pat.

"Who says one can't find any trustworthy help these days? Hmmmph!" the little droid said.

Even if official ceremonies with the Thul family were boring, Jacen thought, meals were not. Their group sat under a soundproof, gravity-controlled dome in a vast room with glossy yellow walls. They all lounged on cushioned benches that surrounded the low toroidal meal table.

In the open center of the table, a food carousel turned slowly to display every kind of fruit, meat, bread, vegetable, sweet, and delicacy Jacen could imagine. At the very center of the carousel bubbled a fountain filled with effervescent blue ossberry ale. Above the soundproof dome, a dozen low-gravity dancers tumbled and pirouetted through the air in the yellow room. But even such a large and wonderful ship as the *Tradewyn* must have seemed like a cage to Aryn and Raynar at the moment, Jacen supposed.

"Mother," Raynar said suddenly, "tell me what you know about Father's disappearance. I've never gotten anything but secondhand reports so far."

Jacen snagged a cluster of orange berries from the food carousel and listened carefully. Aryn pressed her hands tightly together in her lap, and her lively, intelligent face filled with distress. "Bornan said it would be safer if I didn't know about the negotiations he was conducting—some important exchange with a representative of a new political movement. He said that the situation with his contact was quite volatile, but he hoped to have everything smoothed out before the trade conference he would attend on Shumavar."

"He never arrived at the trade conference," Raynar said, filling in the part that he already knew. "But do you know where he went before that? Where was the last place anyone saw him?"

"That much I was able to find out," Aryn said. "Before he disappeared, he was going to some sort of mysterious meeting on an ancient planet called Kuar. Maybe that has something to do with the secret he was hiding."

"Then that's where I need to go to pick up his trail," Raynar said.

"You're not going anywhere, young man," Tyko said. "It's too dangerous. This recent little escapade with Kusk and his brother make that all too clear."

"Kuar," Tenel Ka said from across the table. "An odd place for a meeting, is it not? Has it not been abandoned for centuries?"

"You've heard of the planet, then?" Aryn asked.

"Only by reputation," Tenel Ka said, tossing her red-gold braids behind her shoulders. "Kuar held a small measure of historic interest for me, since it is one of the ancient worlds conquered by Mandalorian warriors. A fearsome race of fighters. I have studied many of their legends."

"Hey, doesn't Boba Fett wear Mandalorian armor?" Jacen said. "And when he found us in the Alderaan system, he was *looking* for Bornan Thul."

"All the more reason to go to Kuar," Raynar said. "My father might have left a message there . . . or at least a clue."

"It's too risky," Aryn said, shaking her head vigorously. "Raynar, if you leave our protection here, a thousand villains will be lying in wait for you."

"Exactly," Tyko added. "If you went to Kuar you could be playing right into some greedy bounty hunter's hands—or worse. Until we can find out what kind of mess my brother has gotten himself into, you and your mother must stay under the protection of the fleet."

"Ah," Tenel Ka said, "aha. But *we* do not need to stay, my friends and I."

"Hey, that's right," Jacen said. "We've got

Tenel Ka's ship, and we can go wherever we want. Nobody will notice us."

Jaina spoke up, looking from Aryn to Raynar. "The four of us could check out Kuar for you—let you know what we find."

Lowie rumbled his approval, and Raynar's eyes lit with hope. "That makes five of us," Em Teedee chimed in.

Above them, one of the low-gravity dancers paused for a moment with her left foot on the top of the dome, then spun off again. Aryn gazed up and watched the dancer drift away. "It's a very kind offer, but I'm afraid I can't let you children—"

"Mother," Raynar interrupted, "they're not children. These are young Jedi Knights. They fought against the Shadow Academy and won."

"Well in that case, *I* think it's an excellent idea," Tyko said. "I need to get back to Mechis III soon, just to check on all the automated systems, or I would make the journey with them myself. The sooner we find out what's happened to Bornan, the sooner we can all get back to leading our own lives." He looked around the table at Jacen, Jaina, Lowie, and Tenel Ka. "The fleet will still be in hiding, but you can report back to me with whatever you find," he said decisively, "and I'll let you know how to contact Raynar and Aryn again."

Raynar looked greatly relieved to have his uncle's support in this. "It's all settled then," he said. "And I'm glad somebody's finally doing something."

"This is a fact," Tenel Ka agreed with a faint smile. "Whenever my pilot and co-pilot are ready, we can leave."

Jaina gulped down the last bit of ossberry ale in her cup, then jumped to her feet. "Well then," she said, "I'm ready for just about anything."

8

EVERYONE WENT THEIR separate ways, but all wanted to see Bornan Thul safely back with his family. Uncle Tyko, confident in the new hyperspace jump randomization program Em Tedee had created, took off for Mechis III in an ornate, boxy ship the color of tarnished brass.

Immediately afterward, with the young Jedi Knights still in the docking bay, the *Tradewyn* and the rest of the hidden Bornaryn fleet made a hyperspace jump. As soon as the jump was complete, the little translating droid began busily "supervising" the *Rock Dragon*'s onboard navicomputer as it calculated the best route to Kuar.

Few things pleased Jaina more in the middle of a crisis than knowing she had a mission—and the means to accomplish it. It felt good to be doing something, to be taking an active part in solving the mystery of Raynar's vanished father. She and Lowie finished their preflight check in record time, while Jacen and Tenel Ka stowed supplies aboard the *Rock Dragon*.

When all of the preparations were finished, Aryn and Raynar came to the big flagship's docking bay to see the companions off. Using a time-delay message transmission, they had already informed Luke Skywalker of the change of plans, and now the *Rock Dragon* was ready to begin the search.

Plainly wishing he could go with his friends, Raynar took slow, deep breaths; Jaina could tell he was doing his best to keep the worry off his face. Lowie, seeing the young man's distress, rumbled a few encouraging words and thumped him on the back with a huge furry hand.

"Don't worry about us, Raynar," Jacen said. "We'll be careful."

"Trust the Force, Raynar," Tenel Ka said. "May it keep you safe."

"You can leave this job to us," Jaina added. "If there's any clue to your father's whereabouts in the ruins of Kuar, we'll pick up the trail." On impulse, she stepped forward and gave him a brief hug, much to Raynar's surprise. Then, to cover her own embarrassment, she gave Aryn a quick hug, too.

"Well," Jaina said gruffly, turning back toward the Hapan passenger shuttle and motioning everyone inside, "what are we waiting for?"

Once they left the merchant fleet behind, Jacen felt a subtle tension building inside him. He felt glad to be going along, but he didn't have a purpose yet on this trip. Jaina and Lowbacca were able to direct their energies into piloting the *Rock Dragon*. Tenel Ka searched for more information about the planet Kuar, punching queries into a datapad on her lap. But Jacen just waited around, with nothing important to do.

He didn't like feeling at a loss. At first he considered just leaning over and reading along on Tenel Ka's datapad, but he rejected that idea, afraid the distraction might annoy her. He had to think of something more substantial to occupy his thoughts.

He didn't want her to think of him as a useless male, as so many of the men on Dathomir and Hapes were considered. He didn't want to think of *himself* that way. He cast about the cockpit looking for some useful task, and his eyes lit on Em Teedee, who was plugged into the navigational control panel.

"Hey, Em Teedee?" he said at last. "As long as we have the time, let's review everything we know about the disappearance of Bornan Thul. Can you keep a list for me?"

"Why certainly, Master Jacen," the translating droid replied cheerfully. "I'm always happy to be of service."

Jaina glanced over her shoulder and flashed her brother a grin. "Good idea. We can all listen in."

Lowie growled the obvious—that Thul's last known destination had been the meeting on Kuar and then he had disappeared en route to Shumavar.

"Point noted," Em Teedee said. "Next?"

"Well, we know he was in the middle of some tricky negotiations," Jacen said. "Something about a political movement. The Diversity Alliance."

"And that he was keeping the subject of those negotiations a complete secret," Jaina added. "Dad was worried about them."

"Excellent," Em Teedee said. "Do go on."

"The Twi'lek woman Nolaa Tarkona was somehow involved in the negotiations," Tenel Ka said.

"Indeed. If I might add a point," Em Teedee said, "in the rubble field of Alderaan we learned from the *Slave IV*'s computer that Boba Fett was hired by Nolaa Tarkona herself. That would imply *she* doesn't know where Bornan Thul is either, so we can logically dismiss the possibility that she somehow captured him or destroyed his ship."

"That makes sense. Nice piece of work, Em Teedee," Jacen said.

Lowie growled the observation that Bornan Thul might have been captured by someone else, or he might be in hiding—or even dead. In any case, it seemed as if half the bounty hunters in the galaxy were out looking for Raynar's father. The Diversity Alliance had offered a lot of credits for the merchant's recovery.

"The price must be high enough to risk dying for," Jaina said with a shudder. "The bounty hunter in the *High Roller* seemed to think so."

Jacen thought for a minute. "All those bounty hunters must be assuming that Bornan Thul disappeared voluntarily and doesn't *want* to be found," he said. "Otherwise, why go to such great lengths to get Raynar and Aryn as hostages?"

"Kusk and his brother must have intended to lure Thul from hiding using his family as bait," Tenel Ka agreed.

"What else do we know?" Jacen mused.

"Well, if Thul *is* hiding, something must have happened to spook him," Jaina observed, "and spook him badly."

In a flash, an idea hit Jacen. "Hey, Em Teedee, access the news reports in the week leading up to the time Bornan Thul disappeared."

"Why certainly, Master Jacen. What sort of news?"

Jacen shrugged. "I'm not sure. Look for anything big or significant that might have happened along the general route Bornan Thul would have taken between Kuar and the trade conference on Shumavar."

"Dear me!" Em Teedee exclaimed. "I

suppose that narrows it down a *bit*, but do you know how many systems there are—?"

"Just do your best," Jacen said.

"I always do, Master Jacen," the droid replied. "One moment . . . ah, here's something," he said. "A double solar eclipse occurred on the fourth planet in the Debray System."

The young Jedi exchanged glances. Finally Jacen said, "I don't think that helps us any. What else do you have?"

Em Teedee made a noise that sounded oddly like gnashing teeth, then continued. "There was a global election on Kath II—" he paused briefly—"notable only for the fact that not a single human was elected to office, although fully one third of Kath's population is human. The Diversity Alliance was campaigning heavily there."

Lowie barked a comment. "Yes, *very* odd," Em Teedee said.

"Probably won't help us in our search, though," Jaina said, raising her eyebrows and waiting.

"Please continue, Em Teedee," Tenel Ka prompted.

"Mmm, odder still," Em Teedee murmured after a short pause to retrieve more data. "It seems that contact was completely lost with an all-human colony on the planet Gammalin. No one has heard from them since the day after Bornan Thul's appointment on Kuar was to have taken place."

"Ah," Tenel Ka said.

"Anything else?" Jacen asked.

"In all probability, yes, Master Jacen," Em Teedee said. "Please be patient. I have fifteen thousand three hundred forty-two other files to search."

Jacen leaned back in his seat and sighed. The trip to Kuar was going to be a long one.

9

WHEN THE *LIGHTNING Rod* arrived at the small colony of Gammalin, Zekk powered up his comm system to request clearance to land. Despite repeated hails, however, he could raise no one. In fact, his ship's scanners detected no signs of life at all on the human settlement. Then again, the sensors hadn't been checked since Zekk's run-in with Boba Fett in the rubble fields of Alderaan. He'd have to have them tuned up when he got to a port with a good mechanic bay. Maybe he could even arrange for Jaina to do it. There were times when he longed to see her again. . . .

The colonists had built only one city on Gammalin, a frontier town. According to its coordinates, the settlement currently lay on the night side of the planet, ap-

proaching morning. But from orbit, Zekk
could spot no city lights when passing over
its position, even with his high-powered
electrobinoculars.

He found this curious. The three-armed
bartender on Borgo Prime had been quite
specific: the missing scavenger Fonterrat
had come *here*. And Zekk's own brief twinges
through the Force told him that Droq'l must
be right. But if so, where *was* everyone?

As he continued to orbit the planet, he
wondered if the city had suffered a massive power outage. Or maybe this was
standard procedure here; a colony strapped
for resources and credits might shut down
all power every night as an austerity measure.

Zekk noted the position of the town on
the edge of the planet's night side. The
local time would be almost morning. In
the absence of any direct communication
from the surface, he began a conservative
standard descent, confident that all his
questions would soon be answered—he
would see for himself.

Gammalin was dry and rocky. Zekk's
instruments indicated a strong breeze that

gusted regularly, moving the dust around. As the *Lightning Rod* cruised over the frontier town, dawn began to break. The sun spilled yellow-gold light across the silent settlement.

Instead of a bustling colony, though, Zekk found only death.

Clusters of weathered prefab buildings lined streets laid out on a precise grid. He spotted no movement, no lights, not even the flicker of candles or torches . . . though he did see several blocks that must have been gutted by a fire raging out of control. It had burned itself out, but there was no evidence that anyone had even tried to stop the fire.

He powered up his comm system and broadcast repeatedly: "Gammalin Colony, this is the *Lightning Rod*—please respond." A tingle ran down his back, echoes of the Force warning him to be cautious. This place did not look right. Did not *feel* right. Had it been abandoned? Entirely evacuated? And if so, why had no one left a beacon?

As he came in lower, Zekk saw the first body lying facedown in the street. Fine dust obscured most of the body, but there was no mistaking that the person was dead.

Now, knowing what to look for, he distinguished other human forms sprawled about, arms and legs akimbo, completely covered by the perpetually blowing dust.

Zekk couldn't believe what he was seeing. He used his scanners as he flew over the entire city, and still detected no signs of life. "Are they *all* dead?" he muttered to himself. Had Fonterrat come here and been killed by whatever had wiped out the rest of this human colony? Maybe there was nothing wrong with the sensors after all.

This was beyond anything in Zekk's previous experience. He set the *Lightning Rod* down in a clearing and prepared to investigate the disaster, feeling compelled to do so. He'd come here merely to find another scavenger—one who might provide a clue to the location of Bornan Thul—and to fulfill his first assignment as a bounty hunter, but now he had one more mystery to solve.

Could Grammalin have been attacked and wiped out by pirates or marauders, perhaps even some leftover Imperial fleet?

He didn't think so. He saw no collateral damage—no blasted buildings, no explosion craters—only the section of burned homes, which could well have been an accidental fire from some heat source left untended.

He shut down the *Lightning Rod*'s engines, but kept them primed just in case he had to leave in great haste. He paused at the exit hatch before unsealing it, afraid of the stench of death he was sure awaited his first breath outside—if the entire population had died, then no one was left to dispose of the bodies.

Zekk froze with his finger on the hatch controls. *Wait! What if this was a virus or bacteria of some kind?* That could explain how everyone had been struck down, why all the buildings seemed abandoned, why no one answered the comm signals. A plague, spreading like wildfire with a hundred percent mortality rate. Zekk shuddered. A disease so horrible it killed everyone . . . and he had almost opened the *Lightning Rod* and breathed in the air!

Zekk went to a supply locker and found an intact environment suit. The *Lightning Rod*'s decontamination systems were still operating efficiently—or at least he hoped so. Peckhum had never known when he might need to sterilize a cargo for transport from one planet to another.

Zekk suited up, tied back his long dark hair, and double-checked the seals on his gloves, on his boots, and around his helmet lock. He took more care than he would have had he been about to step into hard vacuum. Indeed, the creeping plague might well be an even more unpleasant death than the vacuum of space.

Once he stepped outside the ship he could feel the wind rippling gentle fingers across the fabric of his suit. His breathing echoed in his ears, reflecting back inside the helmet so that it sounded as if he were hyperventilating. When he switched on the suit's external voice pickup, he heard only a sighing breeze, like the panting of a grieving parent too exhausted to cry any longer. He heard the hissing of sand and dust being blown around, the groaning of empty buildings, settling houses. But he heard no signs of life. Nothing at all.

He walked along the street. The buildings around him were tall, their windows like blind eyes. He found cadavers sprawled on the street, smothered by drifts of dust. He stood close to one and nudged the sand away with his thick boot, exposing a shriveled, dessicated arm. The skin had turned grayish, peppered with strikingly vivid blotches of blue and green.

He could not bear to uncover the dead man's face, though. Yes, this must be a plague, all right. A terrible plague. As bad as the Death Seed sickness that had struck down so many people years before.

He walked down the street, leaving footprints that were gradually erased by the shifting dust. All around him the dead city seemed eerie, oppressive. He switched on his loudspeaker, turned up the volume, and shouted into the numb air: "Hello! Is anyone alive? Can anyone hear me?"

He listened intently, trying to discern any rustle of movement—some weak survivor crawling to a doorway, hands outstretched for help. Instead, Zekk heard only the echoes of his own words bouncing upward off the abandoned buildings until they were swallowed in the dust-laden sky.

He trudged on down the street, feeling dread. He realized he would never find Fonterrat here . . . at least not alive. And what good would it do him to find the scavenger dead? He did not want to go inside the darkened buildings, which were little more than decaying tombs.

Then, through a gap in the buildings leading to a broad courtyard beyond, he saw a glint of metal not yet covered with dust—a ship! Apparently it had landed not long ago.

As he stopped, he recognized the vessel's configuration, the odd elongated form and ovoid main body. He had seen that vessel among the shards of Alderaan and chased it through the asteroid field, but it had eluded him in the forest of rocks.

Slave IV!

Feeling a sudden sharp tingle of warning, Zekk whirled in his bulky suit and stumbled to one side just as a blaster bolt struck the ground at his feet, fusing the sand into a lump of molten glass. Unable to run in his unwieldy suit, he staggered against a railing outside one of the prefab buildings and saw the helmeted form of Boba Fett stride out from a sheltered doorway.

The bounty hunter pointed his heavy blaster directly at Zekk.

Zekk had a weapon attached to his suit, but he would never be able to draw it in time . . . and he doubted he could shoot faster or more accurately than the fearsome mercenary Boba Fett.

Slowly, he raised both of his gloved hands in surrender. His thoughts whirled as he tried to figure out a way to escape this situation. If Boba Fett recognized Zekk as the one who had shot at him in the asteroid field of Alderaan, the bounty hunter might take great pleasure in eliminating him just for revenge.

"I had thought no one remained alive on this world," Boba Fett said in a rough voice filtered through the speaker in his sealed Mandalorian helmet. "But I see I was wrong. And now you are my captive."

10

"AH. KUAR, FIFTH planet orbiting a single sun in a star system of the same name," Tenel Ka said, reading from her datapad while sitting in one of the crew seats of the Hapan passenger cruiser. "Still capable of sustaining human life, but apparently abandoned for some time . . ."

"Does it say anything about particular cities or structures?" Jaina asked, craning her neck to look out the *Rock Dragon*'s cockpit windowport, peering down toward the unwelcoming landscape below.

"Unfortunately, no," Tenel Ka said, consulting the datapad again.

Lowbacca rumbled a question about the level of technology that might remain on the planet.

"No data on the technology of Kuar's

inhabitants either. In fact," Tenel Ka said, holding up a finger to forestall the question Jacen was about to ask, "other than the legends of the Mandalorian warriors, I have found nothing about the former inhabitants."

Jacen's face fell, then he brightened again. "What about wildlife? Interesting animal species or plants?"

Tenel Ka shook her head grimly. "These files contain minimal data. Little that is of any use to us—only the ramblings of historical scholars speculating about the original inhabitants, before the Mandalorians swept through. None of the data is current. Even planetary archaeologists do not place this site on their priority research lists."

"Hey, Em Teedee, do *you* have any other information about Kuar?" Jacen asked.

"Dear me, I'm afraid to say there's not much, really, aside from what Mistress Tenel Ka has already told you. And I have the coordinates, of course." The little droid made a sound like an aggrieved sigh. "I imagine that's not very useful at this point, is it? We're already here."

"We'll be able to speculate all we want about Kuar in a couple of minutes," Jaina said. "We're almost to the atmosphere. Okay, hit it, Lowie."

The young Wookiee flicked a few switches, and the ship nosed down toward the vast sky that spread its thin blanket over the curved surface of Kuar.

Jaina flashed a conspiratorial grin at her brother and Tenel Ka. "As I always say, show me—don't tell me."

Tenel Ka raised an eyebrow and turned to Jacen. "*Does* she always say that? I have not heard her say it before."

Jacen merely shrugged. The *Rock Dragon* dove into the atmosphere.

The magnified views of the distant landscape below alternated between occasional rock formations and various colors of dust or sand. It seemed as if the dusts of time had sifted over the entire world. But excitement had overtaken Jacen, and he was impatient to know more about the mysterious place beneath them. "Hey, what do the readings say?" he asked.

"Life-forms," Jaina answered succinctly. "Quite a few, in fact. Definitely non-human—at least the life-forms we're picking up right now."

Lowie gave a thoughtful purr. "Quite right, Master Lowbacca," Em Teedee said. "There's no telling yet whether the life-forms are sentient or not."

A few thin clouds drifted high in the atmosphere like worn and tattered lace, but they did little to obstruct Jacen's view through the windowport. From this height, the surface seemed relatively flat and featureless. "What about buildings?" he asked.

Lowie studied the readouts again and woofed a few times. "Most assuredly, Master Lowbacca. Those are definitely not natural formations," Em Teedee said. "I'd hardly call them *buildings*, however. The structures are certainly old, but there's something odd about them—irregular, as if they're only half there."

"Ruins, perhaps?" Tenel Ka suggested.

"Quite probably," Em Teedee agreed.

"Why don't we just get closer and see?" Jacen asked impatiently. "That's the best way to find out."

Jaina sighed. "I purposely stayed high, in hopes that we'd spot a city or smuggler's encampment, or pick up a beacon of some sort to show us where any inhabited areas might be. I thought it would be the easiest way to figure out where Bornan Thul might have gone. You're right, though—we'll have to go down closer."

Jacen grinned at her, raising his eyebrows. "Well, what are you waiting for?"

She took the *Rock Dragon* lower until they were skimming just two hundred meters above the surface. In most areas, the vegetation was fairly sparse. Rocky spikes and pillars and mesas jutted up from the landscape. Occasionally, Jacen saw what looked like a nest of some sort on one of the outcroppings. The color of the dirt, sand, and rock varied from cream, to saffron, to gray, to pale blue with purplish striations, to bright ochre, to stark obsidian.

Lowie woofed and tapped the control panel in front of him.

"Yep, I see it," Jaina said.

"What kind of structures?" Jacen asked.

"I'm afraid I can't say," Em Teedee replied. "They are approximately three kilometers ahead of us. At least that's what the ship's sensors indicate."

"There," Jaina said as she slowed the *Rock Dragon* and dropped even lower. The thick wall that surrounded the small city atop a high, strategic hill was broken in several places. Some of the buildings inside the enclosure seemed in good repair, but others were cracked and crumbling. A variety of furred and feathered creatures bounded, scurried, or swooped from building to building. Yellow, six-legged reptiles with curly tails clung to the sunny side of every wall or turret.

"No people," Tenel Ka observed.

"Somebody must live on this planet. Maybe they just don't like this city for some reason," Jacen said. "The others might still be inhabited, though." He wished they could stop to explore, so he could study the strange creatures he had just seen, but Jaina pulled the *Rock Dragon* up and had already begun looking for the next city. They flew for hours across the surface of the planet, zigzagging back and forth to cover more ground. They came upon a score of other ghost cities, fortresses, and villages in varying states of disrepair. None were inhabited, and none had been disturbed in centuries. Civilization on Kuar had died out long ago, and it seemed that no new settlers had taken up residence here.

They found no clues to Bornan Thul's

whereabouts, no evidence to show he or anyone else, had been here.

Jacen was beginning to get nervous. He could see Jaina biting her lower lip. "Where *are* people when you need them?" he heard her mutter.

"You, um . . . you don't suppose," Jacen began, "that some war or virus or something could have killed everybody on Kuar, do you?"

Jaina darted him a startled look, as if she had not thought of this.

"No," Tenel Ka said simply. "The Mandalorians used the planet briefly after they conquered it. Then they abandoned this place."

"Rest assured, Master Jacen," Em Teedee chimed in, "all evidence indicates that the settlements we're seeing have been deserted for hundreds—if not thousands—of years."

Jacen relaxed slightly. "Okay, there aren't any people. Then what exactly are we looking for, anyway?"

"No people, no beacons, . . ." Jaina mused. "Where would strangers plan to meet? A landmark maybe?" Jaina said.

"There is much surface area to cover," Tenel Ka pointed out.

"It would have to be an obvious meeting place, then," Jaina said. "Something that's easy to find on a planet this size."

Lowie rumbled that the meeting place would need a good landing area nearby.

"Okay, that's what we're looking for, then." Jaina nodded. "Trust me, I'll know it when I see it."

Jacen, Lowie, and Tenel Ka exchanged amused glances.

As it turned out, Jaina was right. Just before dawn she saw a broad-based mesa that rose a kilometer above the cracked and dusty plain. As they drew closer, it became clear that the plateau, which was close to three kilometers wide, was not really a mesa. The majority of the mountain's flat top had collapsed into a deep crater, surrounded by an artificially broad, level rim, forming a gigantic natural arena.

Houses and tunnels and walkways and stairs had long ago been built into the interior sides of the crater. From the floor of the crater rose the ruins of a vast array of tall, crumbling buildings. A network of rusty chains connected the tops of these structures, like the web design of some deranged insect. Jaina brought the *Rock*

Dragon in for a smooth landing on the broad lip of the crater.

"Here we are," she said smugly. "Landmark. Easy to spot. Excellent landing area. This would be my guess." Lowie agreed enthusiastically.

"Our sensors indicate no signs of airborne contaminants that would endanger the lives of humans or Wookiees," Em Teedee assured them. "The atmosphere is perfectly breathable."

"Everybody out, then," Jaina said. "Time to stretch our legs."

"Great," Jacen sighed, unbuckling his crash webbing. He was already thinking about what kinds of unusual creatures they might encounter, hoping he would find some of the interesting specimens he had seen from the air.

"Now the next stage of our search begins," Tenel Ka said. "The real work." She followed Jacen down the shuttle's exit ramp, breathing deeply of the dry air. Jaina and Lowie tumbled after them, eager to move about after their long journey.

Jacen ran to the edge of the deep crater and looked down at the patchwork of ancient buildings, chains, and walls dappled by shadows. "It could take a long time to search all that," he said. "It's a whole city."

Lowie gave a negative growl. "Lowie's right. I think it would be more logical to start up here," Jaina said. "The best place to set down a ship would be somewhere along this rim," she made a sweeping gesture with one arm to indicate the wide ledge that encircled the crater, "rather than down there."

After a brief consultation, the young Jedi Knights spread out from the rocky edge and spaced themselves to cover the greatest area. They walked slowly around the rim, scanning the ground ahead and to each side for any sign of a recent disturbance in the ancient settled dust.

After several false alarms—which turned out to be nothing more than a gouge out of the rock, a shiny feather, or some animal droppings—Jacen, who was closest to the outer rim, saw something flutter up ahead. Shading his eyes with one hand against the direct glare of the early morning sun, he ran forward, certain in his heart that he had discovered something important. To his great disappointment, though, he found nothing more than a flat gray slab of rock, as large as one of the serving trays back at the Jedi academy. His sister, Lowie, and Tenel Ka dashed up beside him.

"What is it?" Jaina asked.

"Nothing, I guess," Jacen said. "I thought I saw something colorful moving over here—fluttering, kind of. Maybe it was just a bird or a plume of dust, I don't know."

Tenel Ka bent low and circled the rock. "Ah. Aha," she said. She reached beneath the edge and pulled. "Lowbacca, my friend—?" she began, but before she could finish her request, Lowie had already lifted the slab of rock high overhead and tossed it aside down the steep edge inside the crater. Tenel Ka straightened. In her hand she held a long piece of cloth, a sash, sewn from alternating strips of yellow, purple, red, and orange fabric. "The colors of the House of Thul," she said matter-of-factly. "Raynar's mother also wore such a sash."

"Why, bless me," Em Teedee exclaimed. He was viewing the scene from a perspective that none of the others had. "Does the House of Thul also place inscriptions on its clothing?"

"Not that I've ever noticed," Jacen said,

wondering what the little droid was getting at.

"May I see that?" Jaina asked. Tenel Ka handed her the sash. Jaina grasped the material with one hand near each end and stretched it out straight. She scanned the sash, then flipped it over. "Look!"

Jacen moved closer. Sure enough, there on the yellow band of material scratched in faint gray letters was a message.

"*Danger,*" it said. "*If I am caught, all humans in mortal danger. Thul.*"

"Gracious me!" Em Teedee exclaimed. "If this warning is genuine, then I do hope Master Thul is safe. If not, we're doomed!"

11

UNDER THE HAZY midmorning sunshine of Kuar, Jacen stood with the other young Jedi Knights outside the *Rock Dragon*. They talked earnestly, waiting until all ideas had been discussed to make their decision. It reminded Jacen of those political meetings his mother always complained about . . . but now he saw the necessity for careful planning. Considering the ominous message on the sash, he and Jaina, Tenel Ka, and Lowie needed to be certain their next step in the quest to find Raynar's father was a prudent one.

"Well, we know he came here," Jacen said, "and had some kind of important meeting, then left that warning written on his sash."

Tenel Ka nodded, her warrior braids

swinging like red-gold chains. "Yes, and the business Bornan Thul transacted must be connected with his disappearance."

Jaina paced on the weathered ground. "But what was it? And why did they come to *this* planet? Is Kuar just an out-of-the-way meeting place—or was there some connection to the ancient Mandalorians?"

Jacen rubbed his hands together and grinned eagerly. "Hey, I think we should explore those ruins some more. There's plenty of places we haven't looked into. Who knows what clues we might still find?"

Lowie growled, his fur ruffling. Em Teedee translated. "Yes indeed—and who knows what vicious creatures we might find?"

Jacen bobbed his head, still grinning. "Yeah, just think!"

Holding on to the thick rusted chains, careful to avoid the broken staircases and treacherous ramps, the young Jedi Knights made their way down the cliff wall into the stadium. Out in the hazy distance, clouds of dust hung like brown soup in the air. The bowl-shaped crater had once been the home of towering buildings, a crowded and sheltered city. Later, the Mandalorians had turned the entire crater into a fighting arena. Now, though, the forgotten metropolis lay abandoned and decaying, filled with thousands upon thousands of years of unrecorded history.

The companions worked their way along open galleries gouged into the cliff. Tenel Ka pointed out that the Mandalorians had allowed spectators to watch violent gladiatorial combats from such galleries. But it looked as if no spectator had sat in these stands for half the age of the galaxy, and the Mandalorian warriors who had once made their homes here had long since moved on in their endless nomadic conquests.

In the shadowed interiors of alcoves and stadium rooms, Jacen marveled at the immense outgrowths of shelf fungus, colored pale pink and lavender and peach; some mushrooms formed circular platforms, while others rose up in conical spikes like stalagmites. Centipedelike insects burrowed through the foamy flesh of the fungus, making miniature warrens.

Jaina studied the scuffed dust around

their feet. "Looks like something moved through here not long ago."

Jacen perked up. "Do you think it might have been Raynar's father—or whoever he was meeting here?"

"This is difficult to determine. The prints are blurred," Tenel Ka said, bending down. "The tracks could be human . . . or some other creature. We must be cautious."

"You're *always* cautious, Tenel Ka," Jacen said. "It's one of the things I like about you."

"There's certainly a great deal to be said for being cautious, Master Jacen," Em Teedee intoned.

Jaina turned her glowrod toward an arched opening to a passage that led deeper into the cliffside. "This looks like a main tunnel," she said. Her light splashed on a fallen pillar and rooms filled with crumbling rock from collapsed ceilings and walls.

The scuffed tracks led deeper into the tunnel, and Jacen scratched his tousled brown hair, trying to imagine why Bornan Thul would have gone inside this chamber. Had some precious artifact been hidden here, away from prying eyes? What was he after, and why would it spell doom for all humans if he was caught with it?

Inside the passage, shadows clung to them like a blanket soaked in oil. They pushed onward, clustering close to Jaina's glowrod. "Master Lowbacca," Em Teedee said, "would you be so kind as to reposition me? I'm afraid my optical sensors are picking up nothing more than the rock wall of the tunnel. From this angle I can't even add to the level of illumination in here."

Lowbacca sniffed the sluggish, stale air, growled low in his throat, and reached down to move Em Teedee to a better position on his syren-fiber belt.

"I will provide us with more light as well," Tenel Ka said. She removed her lightsaber and gripped its intricately carved bone-white handle. She pushed the power stud, and her brilliant turquoise energy beam flashed out like a javelin made of light, dazzling them all.

Just then the monster struck.

The creature charged toward them, a huge battering ram of spined legs, jointed footpads, an armored body core, and fangs . . . many fangs. The thing seemed as large as an Imperial scout walker.

"Oh, do look out!" Em Teedee said.

Tenel Ka leaped in front of the beast as the other young Jedi Knights fell back, scrambling for their lightsabers.

Jacen tried to focus his dazzled eyes as the glistening creature thundered forward. A bone-jarring roar emanated from a gullet deep behind its clacking jaws. The monster was spiderlike and enormous; spines like wicked thorns sprouted from every joint. Its body core was crimson, splotched with a jagged marking on its back that looked like a death's-head.

Jacen recognized the creature. "I think that's a combat arachnid," he said. "They're very rare and very deadly. I never thought I'd get to see one."

"Aren't we lucky," Jaina said. She drew her own lightsaber, but Tenel Ka was bearing the brunt of the creature's attention.

The warrior girl held her lightsaber upright, her jaw set, her face grim. She swept the blade back and forth, ripping a gash of light through the air. "Stay back!" she snarled.

The monster reached out with a long clawed foreleg, trying to grab Tenel Ka, but she slashed low, slicing off its footpad. The creature bellowed and reared back, jabbing its spined legs at her like an armful of lances. Slashing again, the warrior girl drove in and severed another of its many legs.

Lowbacca ignited his molten bronze lightsaber with a roar of challenge, and stepped forward.

"Do we have to kill it?" Jacen said, trying to think of an alternative.

Drool slathered the combat arachnid's grinding jaws, and its many bulbous eyes looked like black pearls reflecting the lines of light that danced over its polished exoskeleton.

Jaina said, "This is one creature you're not taking home as a pet, Jacen."

Reluctantly lighting his emerald-green lightsaber, he stood ready to fight beside his friends.

Teeth bared, Lowbacca planted himself next to Tenel Ka, swinging his lightsaber like a club. He nipped off several sharp spines that rose from the combat arachnid's back, but one of the creature's forelimbs flashed out and tore into his fur, making the young Wookiee stagger backward.

"Didn't I tell you to be careful, Master

Lowbacca?" Em Teedee scolded. Lowie roared in pain as he looked at the shallow wound along his rib cage.

Jaina chopped away another flailing leg, but the combat arachnid had too many limbs—and now it was angered and in pain. The beast pressed them back, trapping them between a pile of fallen rock and the wall.

"Uh-oh, looks like we can't get out," Jacen said. He stood in front of his sister, his green lightsaber held high, but the combat arachnid swatted him aside, knocking him into Tenel Ka. In the instant the warrior girl lost her balance, the creature struck. It grabbed Tenel Ka and lifted her up into the air, ready to kill her.

"No!" Jacen cried. "Tenel Ka!" He tried to reach the monster's mind through the Force, but the creature reared up and trumpeted a challenge.

Bellowing, Lowie charged into the fray. The enraged combat arachnid knocked him backward, its spined limbs jabbing like sharp spears in every direction. Its jaws clacked together, ready to shred flesh from Tenel Ka's bones.

Jacen didn't think he could attack in

time to save his friend. The creature was too powerful. It could sustain a great deal of damage and many more wounds before it suffered a mortal injury. Jacen drew a deep breath, determined to attack anyway.

Just then, Jacen saw a movement in the opening out into the sunlight. A tall hairy silhouette appeared. It let out a deep-throated, yet somehow melodious, Wookiee roar and fired a powerful blaster rifle. The dazzling energy bolt splashed across the combat arachnid's lower set of eyes; another blast followed, and a third struck the remaining eyes on the spider creature.

The combat arachnid's thick shell was too strong to be split open by a mere hand weapon, but the creature hissed and flailed. With a shuddering spasm it dropped Tenel Ka and backed up against the wall, its jointed forelimbs writhing and clawing at its eyes.

The female Wookiee voice growled, and Jacen, who was closest, could hear enough of the words to understand the message with his meager grasp of the Wookiee language.

"It's temporarily blinded," he translated.

"We've got to get out of here before it recovers and attacks us again."

"No argument from me," Jaina said, picking herself up. Lowie, pressing a hairy paw to his injured side, staggered away from the battleground. His hand rapidly became covered with blood.

Jacen helped a stunned but otherwise uninjured Tenel Ka to stand, pulling her arm around his shoulder so that he could walk outside with her.

As they returned to the wan sunlight, Jacen got a good look at the tall chocolate-brown Wookiee, a female wearing a tattered weapons belt to which were clipped many sonic grenades and thermal detonators. Lowbacca stopped and stared at her, absolutely stricken. He groaned. Jacen could tell that Lowie had said no actual words: he had merely voiced an expression of amazement and disbelief.

The female Wookiee spoke again, and Em Teedee bleeped in surprise, recognizing the name. "Raabakyysh? Master Lowbacca are you saying that this is your deceased Wookiee friend from Kashyyyk—the one who disappeared in the deepest levels of the forest?"

Jacen gasped. "Blaster bolts! This is *Raaba*? You mean she's not dead after all? How did you escape?"

"Uh, can we talk about it later?" Jaina urged, throwing a glance over her shoulder.

With a noncommital grunt, the female Wookiee gestured for them to hurry. They ran after her, knowing there would be time for questions, many questions, after they were safe.

Once the combat arachnid was a good distance behind them, Jacen let himself become engrossed in speculation about what had happened to Lowbacca's dear friend and where she had been for all this time.

12

IN HER PRIVATE chambers connected to the throne-room grotto, Nolaa Tarkona sat at a long polished table carved out of lava rock. Though the day outside was broiling hot in one direction and disastrously cold in the other, the Ryloth cave warrens remained at a pleasant, constant temperature. Dimness was an ever-present companion.

Across from her, Adjutant Advisor Hovrak shuffled his paraphernalia, preparing for his daily presentation. The Shistavanen wolfman stared at the electronic datapad on which he kept the most secret records of the Diversity Alliance. With clawed fingers Hovrak punched buttons, calling up entries in his encyclopedia of alien species.

Nolaa watched with interest—the records had become an obsession with the wolfman. Holographic images gelled into focus from his catalog, and the Adjutant Advisor discussed their progress, referring to the new entries he had compiled.

The sharp image of a broad-shouldered, long-limbed cyclops rotated to show the brute's features from 360 degrees. "An Abyssin," said Hovrak. "Not very smart, but violent and brutal. Once trained, they are great fighters. We have quite a few already in our ranks, and I believe that with a little effort we could get most of their species to join the Diversity Alliance."

Nolaa nodded, taking in the information as Hovrak called up the next entry. "Cha'a, a small reptilian species."

She saw a squat creature, its head mounted low on its shoulders as if its neck had retracted into its spine. The slitted eyes were set wide apart. Delicate scales covered a sloping head that looked like a snake's.

"Wily, ambitious, untrustworthy—though the Cha'a can be counted on to look after their own interests."

Nolaa nodded, tapping a claw against her newly resharpened teeth. "Then we must convince them that being loyal to the Diversity Alliance *is* in their best interests."

"My thoughts exactly," Hovrak said with a snarl. "Several Cha'a have been tricked into joining Luke Skywalker's Jedi training center, but I believe most have no great love for humans and their domination."

Nolaa stroked her one intact head-tail, feeling the tingle of sensations. She had tattooed designs across the smooth, greenish flesh. The stuttering pain of the tattoo needles had been excruciating on the intensely sensitive skin of her brain appendage, every touch of the ink-filled stinger needles a throb of painful exhilaration, and she had endured it. Few Twi'lek males could tolerate such prolonged agony—and now everyone who saw her tattoos could not help but admire her endurance. It added to her power.

Nolaa's other head-tail, which had once been so long, so supple, so beautiful, had been blasted off in the violent battle when she had overthrown her slave master, killed him and his henchmen, then made her escape.

Although losing a head-tail was a severe handicap to Twi'leks, Nolaa Tarkona had survived. In the twitching stump she had implanted an optical sensor that could pick up images from behind and relay them to her brain, thus increasing her deadly mystique. This Twi'lek woman who had overthrown a male-dominated culture, slaughtered her masters, and launched a powerful political movement literally had an eye in the back of her head. . . .

"Chevin," Hovrak continued, "a species easily recognized by their startlingly long faces and huge heads." The display showed a creature whose chin hung down nearly to its ankles. "Many humans find them unsavory, particularly ugly, but the Chevin view themselves as opportunistic realists interested in their own well-being."

Nolaa smiled. "We are interested in the well-being of *all* alien peoples."

Hovrak pointed to the image on the datapad. "Unfortunately, we still have no representatives from this species, despite our propaganda campaign."

"Then I believe we ought to work harder to recruit at least one Chevin," Nolaa said with a faint frown. "Even if it takes a bribe."

"Yes," Hovrak said, growling deep in his

throat. Nolaa Tarkona's disappointment in his failure to recruit a Chevin came as a personal defeat to Hovrak. "I believe I shall concentrate my efforts on that species."

A Gamorrean guard strode in and stood snuffling at attention. Because they were intensely loyal and able to follow orders, so long as they were simple enough, Nolaa had found the porcine guards to be good henchmen. She didn't for a minute expect that they might betray her; they were too stupid to think of such a thing.

"Lunch ready," the Gamorrean said in a phlegm-filled voice.

Hovrak froze the image on the datapad and stood up, his fur bristling. "Good, I'm ready for food, fresh food . . . *wet food*." He snarled in anticipation, flexing his claws.

Deciding to stretch her legs as well, Nolaa followed the wolfman out to the main grotto, where holding cells dotted the walls. "Another newly arrived prisoner?" she asked.

Saliva had already begun to run in the wolfman's mouth. "Yes, a fresh one—fresh from Concord Dawn, convicted of cheating at Sabacc."

"Cheating at Sabacc, nothing more?" Nolaa said. "And they sent him to *you*?"

"On Concord Dawn, cheating is a capital offense." Hovrak's black lips curled back away from his fangs. "And laws are laws." Moving with stiff, tensely coiled muscles, as if he were stalking prey, Hovrak strode toward one of the cell doors. "Besides," he snarled back over his shoulder, "one of the senior magistrates there, a Devaronian, is sympathetic to our cause."

He opened the cell door, clenching and unclenching his clawed hands.

From inside the prison chamber a weak voice, a deliciously *human* voice, wailed, "Please let me go! I'm innocent. I didn't know cheating was a capital offense. I'll never do it again!"

Hovrak merely snarled. The voice changed abruptly in tone.

"Wait, what are you doing? Stop. Noooo!"

The human voice ended in a gurgling scream. Then one of the Gamorrean guards slammed the cell door so that Nolaa didn't have to listen to the wet, tearing sounds as the wolfman ate his lunch.

Nolaa waited patiently. She decided not to take a meal now. Not yet. She usually ate alone in her private chambers, dining on food she prepared herself. It was a habit she had developed . . . not that she expected any members of the Diversity Alliance to poison her. No, she knew how fiercely loyal they were. She just liked it better that way. More self-sufficient.

Nolaa would have liked to dine with her half-sister . . . if lovely Oola had survived to see these glory days. Nolaa Tarkona had brought supreme triumph to the Twi'leks . . . and especially to females of the species. But not before her half-sister had been captured as a slave, her teeth sanded flat, her memories of family and clan hammered out of her. Poor, innocent Oola had been brainwashed, stripped, beaten. Her entire life had become one of servitude—dancing and otherwise pleasing the whims of those who had paid to own her, body and soul.

Twi'lek dancing girls were highly prized throughout the galaxy. One of the despicable criminals of their own species, Bib Fortuna, had cast his lot in with the highest bidder and acted as a simpering henchman to a crime lord, with no pride in himself or in his people. Fortuna had purchased Oola and other dancing girls, dragging them against their will to serve Jabba the Hutt. Oola had served indeed, and served well.

Nolaa had dug deep to find details of her half-sister's time in the Hutt's palace, even receiving spy-holo images of how well Oola had danced, the grace with which she moved, her greenish skin glistening with sweat, her head-tails flying about like the wind in a storm. Oola had given the Hutt everything he wanted—until one day, on a whim, Jabba had fed her to his pet rancor. The imprisoned monster had devoured Nolaa's dear half-sister in much the same way that Hovrak now snacked on the hapless scam artist in the cell. Ah well. At least the scam artist was a mere *human*.

Nolaa felt a twinge of sadness at the memory of her half-sister, imagining how, together, they could have proven themselves to the galaxy at large. But soon she let the grief turn to anger. Nolaa had always found anger to be a more productive emotion anyway.

Finally, the wolfman emerged from the cell, wiping blood spatters from his muzzle and his fur with a self-moistened napkin.

Then he tossed it away, along with the stained apron he had worn to protect his Diversity Alliance uniform. He meticulously combed his black-brown hair and, using a long claw to pick a shred of food from between his sharp teeth, straightened his Adjutant Advisor uniform again. "Now then, Esteemed Tarkona, shall we return to work?"

"Yes," Nolaa said, stroking her single head-tail and walking back to the private meeting chambers. "We have only a standard hour until I must depart for the grand campaign on Chroma Zed. If we do our work properly there, we can gain converts throughout that system."

"Let's hope so," the wolfman said. "I don't believe the Chromans are on our list yet."

They returned to the private chamber, and Hovrak punched his electronic datapad again. "Now then, let's see . . ." Another alien appeared in the holographic projector, a blue-skinned goatlike creature with a trio of eyes on stalks protruding from its forehead.

"The Grans, easily distinguishable by their three eyes. Traditionally unreliable, easily bribed, and quickly addicted to drugs or liquors . . . but shrewd and often underestimated. If we could recruit several, they could infiltrate the seediest cantinas in the galaxy. . . ."

The Adjutant Advisor continued through the alphabet.

13

RAABA SPRINTED AHEAD on her long Wookiee legs, leading the way to safety as they fled up broken ramps and half-collapsed staircases in the honeycombed warrens of the cliffside stadium. A network of sagging chains draped across the dust-filled crater, connecting to weathered build-ingtops in a sinister high-wire network.

Raaba cinched her ragged headband, once bright red but now faded to a dusty carmine, more tightly around her forehead. She chuffed at them to hurry and contin-ued to lope through alternating islands of sunlight and barricades of shadows.

"Dear me, all this running is beginning to jiggle my circuits loose," Em Teedee said. "I do wish we could pause so that Raabakyysh could explain a few things. I'm most curious

133

to know why she would allow poor Master Lowbacca to believe she was dead all this time."

Just then, a series of clattering, rustling noises came from several cliffside tunnels, like the ghostly echoes of long-departed spectators at the great gladiatorial games. . . . No. Like marching insectile feet with sharp claws and hard body armor.

"Then again, explanations can wait," the little translating droid said. "I propose that we make getting to safety our highest priority!"

"Sounds like more combat arachnids," Jacen said, panting and puffing as he ran. "Lots and lots of them. This place must be infested."

"I thought you said they were rare creatures," Jaina snorted. "They're a bit too common for me right now."

"Hey, it's not my fault!" Jacen said. "They *are* rare. But combat arachnids were bred for showcase battles in arenas like this one. So I'm guessing that a bunch of them were brought here for exhibition fights. These're probably feral descendants of the victorious ones left by the Mandalorians when they abandoned this world."

"Survival of the fittest?" Tenel Ka said,

her granite-gray eyes flashing at Jacen. "They seem fit enough to hunt for their own food—us!"

"Don't worry, Tenel Ka. I won't let any of them get you again," he said. She raised an eyebrow at the very suggestion that she would require anyone to protect her now, and kept running.

Lowie turned around and snarled when he heard something else approach. Something threatening. He pressed a paw against the bleeding gash in his side, ignoring the pain of the wound as he sniffed the air.

As Jacen turned to look, three combat arachnids scurried out of the shadows *in front of them*, mandibles clacking, deadly spines extended, positioned to fight as a predatory team.

"They're in front of us! We're doomed!" Em Teedee said.

A moment later, two more combat arachnids boiled out of the chambers behind them, trapping the companions along the walkway precipice that looked out upon the sprawling crater.

"Oh, no! We're double-doomed," the little droid wailed.

Raaba held her battered blaster in front of her. Jacen and Jaina, Tenel Ka, and

Lowie each powered up their lightsabers again.

Raaba growled and looked meaningfully, almost apologetically, at Lowbacca, as if she hoped to live long enough to give him all the explanations he desired. She gestured across the bowl of the crater to the broken buildingtops where her ship, a small interstellar skimmer, waited on one flat rooftop. Thick, dangling chains stretched out from the wall across the yawning gulf, connecting to the distant tower. The chocolate-furred Wookiee bellowed and pointed urgently.

"You want us to climb . . . out *there*?" Jacen said.

Tenel Ka strode to the thick corroded chain and grasped it with her one arm. "You can use the Force to help you balance, my friend Jacen," she said. "If you concentrate, it will be no worse than walking on a forest path."

"Forest path, huh?" Jacen asked with a gulp. "Sure. No problem."

Raaba bounded onto the chain as the combat arachnids stuttered forward from both directions, their pointed limbs flailing, multiple eyes blazing with hunger.

Lowie bellowed and lunged back at the creatures, sweeping his molten bronze lightsaber in a broad arc. He lopped off three limbs from the nearest creature as if they were stalks of grain.

The combat arachnid shrieked and staggered backward into one of its companions. The second, already-enraged monster struck out at the stumbling, wounded arachnid—and the two creatures began to rip at each other. Greenish clots of blood flew through the air.

The other arachnids ignored the distraction, however, and drove in for the kill, focused on their intended victims.

Tenel Ka stood easily on the rusty chain, legs spread, perfectly balanced in her glittering lizard-hide armor. She reached down and grabbed hold of Jacen. "Come, my friend, I will assist you."

"Hey, thanks!" he gasped. "To show my appreciation, I'll tell you a joke when all this is over, okay?"

"That will not be necessary," the warrior girl answered quickly. "Please—I require no such expression of gratitude."

With fluid Wookiee grace, Raaba began to sprint across the incredible drop as if the sagging chain were a rope bridge. Her heavy footsteps sent jolting vibrations along the links, and even with the Force, it was all Jacen could do to maintain his balance. He crept along one tiny step at a time. Jaina climbed up after him.

Lowbacca, agile from climbing trees and vines for most of his life on Kashyyyk, easily brought up the rear. He moved backward along the chain, still pressing one hand against his wound and holding his lightsaber with the other.

Unfortunately, the thick chains and the perilous height did not deter the combat arachnids. The spined carnivorous creatures clambered onto the chain as if it were a web they had spun.

When the companions had scrambled about halfway to where Raaba's ship had landed, Lowie bellowed an order. Em Teedee called to the others, "Master Lowbacca urges you to increase your speed, although I myself would suggest that you also exercise extreme caution."

"We're being careful, Em Teedee. Don't worry," Jacen said, easing forward a couple of steps.

"That is most reassuring, Master Jacen. However, I still reserve the right to express concern about your well-being."

As if to make Em Teedee's point, a cold, dry breeze picked up, howling in the open air. Jacen wobbled. "Blaster bolts!" he said, windmilling his arms to stabilize himself. The chains creaked and swayed beneath him. "I'm not sure this is such a good idea."

"Maybe not," Jaina answered, glancing at the chasm below them, "but falling down there is an even worse idea. So what are we waiting for?"

Although the combat arachnids moved more slowly along the chains than the agile Wookiees, they might still be able to catch up with the humans before they reached safety. Realizing this, Lowie held his ground, wrapping his Wookiee feet around the links of the chain, bending his hairy knees, and holding his lightsaber up to defend his friends from attack. He gestured with his claws extended, urging them to go on ahead without him.

Raaba grunted encouragement to him and increased her speed, leading the way. Tenel Ka followed, keeping her careful balance, but Jacen had trouble following as quickly. Jaina held both of her hands out to steady herself.

They crept forward as quickly as they dared, desperately making their way toward Raaba's ship, and possible rescue.

One of the horrible creatures finally reached Lowbacca, and he met it with his lightsaber. The combat arachnid reared up, using several legs to maintain its balance. Its crimson body core glinted menacingly under the hazy sun of Kuar.

Lowie slashed with his lightsaber, but the arachnid dodged sideways, eluding the beam. In a counterstrike, it swept out a segmented leg and caught the ginger-furred Wookiee with the tip of one footpad. The blow knocked him backward—and Lowie toppled off the thick chain. Jacen and Jaina both screamed.

At the last instant, though, Lowie reached out with his free arm and grabbed one of the heavy metal links of chain. He swung beneath it, using his momentum to bring him up and around to the other side of the combat arachnid. As the creature stretched down to snatch at him, like a fisher trying to scoop a meal from a stream, Lowie grasped one of the arachnid's stable rear legs and used it to haul himself back up onto the chain.

The arachnid turned, trumpeting its outrage. Lowie swung his lightsaber like a club and cleaved a long gash through the center of the monster's eye cluster. The creature roared and thrashed, spewing venomous saliva from its mouth hole.

It took all of Lowie's strength to evade the arachnid's attack and reach its body core. Then, with a great growl he shoved the monster off the thick chain. It flailed its many legs as it fell down, down, *down*, until it splattered in a starburst pattern far below at the bottom of the crater.

Lowie scrambled backward, getting to his feet and regaining his balance again as the other combat arachnids hesitated, wary now that they had seen their Wookiee foe emerge triumphant from battle with one of their kind.

Raaba finally reached the other end of the chain where it was anchored to the high rooftop. She sprang from the chain and stood waiting, ready to offer her help to the young Jedi Knights.

Tenel Ka moved to the anchor point and stopped to extend her hand to Jacen as he inched toward her, trying not to look down. Lowie's wrestling match with the combat arachnid had made the chain bounce and shake so much that Jacen and Jaina had been forced to spend most of their concentration on not falling, rather than making forward progress.

Now, though, as they neared the dubious safety of the rooftop and Raaba's ship, Lowie began bounding toward them along the chain, running with uncanny balance to catch up. The two combat arachnids that had not yet given up the chase scrambled after him, hissing and clicking, ravenous for fresh food.

Raaba yanked one of the small detonators from her criss crossed ammunition belt, set the timer, and without pausing lobbed it in a perfect arc. The detonator sailed across the open air.

Seeing the glittering object, the foremost combat arachnid reared up to catch it, as if the thermal detonator might be some sort of flying prey. The grenade detonated, shattering the creature's exoskeleton like a thousand chips of glass, spraying its innards in all directions.

The shock wave from the explosion hurled Jacen sideways. He spun, grabbed for balance, and then slipped from the chain—but Tenel Ka's arm shot out like lightning to seize him by the elbow and halt his terrible fall.

Spurred by the thought of all that open air below, Jacen and Tenel Ka drew on the Force together to bring him back up again. Then the two of them, along with Jaina, finally scrambled to the sturdy rooftop, where it was safe . . . almost.

The final combat arachnid, seeing its prey about to escape, increased its speed. It hissed and scrabbled along the chain, climbing like a deadly acrobat.

Lowie bounded ahead, ignoring the gusts of wind, planting his feet firmly from one link to the next. The last combat arachnid closed the gap, its jaws clacking. Lowie could not look behind him to fight. His best chance was to reach the rooftop before the creature could grab hold of him. The wound in his side was bleeding profusely now, but the young Wookiee didn't seem to notice.

"Come on, Lowie!" Jacen cried. "You can make it!"

With a final burst of speed, Lowbacca leaped the final several meters to the rooftop. The last combat arachnid charged forward like a landspeeder out of control—but Tenel Ka thought quickly, efficiently.

In a flash of blazing turquoise, she swept

her lightsaber downward to sever the ancient metal links that anchored the chain to the rooftop.

Just as the combat arachnid reached out to grab for the companions, the chain broke free and fell away with the monster still clinging to it. The heavy links of corroded durasteel plummeted, carrying the unwilling passenger down, down, until it struck the far side of the amphitheater wall with enough force to squash the multi-legged creature.

His heart pounding, Jacen was relieved to see how isolated they were on this skyscraper, away from the walls of the great crater.

Lowie slumped to the rooftop, shaking and exhausted. Raaba came over, put her arm around his shoulder, and gave him a powerful hug. She touched the wound on his side with a groan of concern, then went to her ship to rummage for a medikit. Lowie looked up at her, his eyes filled with a thousand questions.

"My, that *was* exciting, wasn't it?" Em Teedee said.

14

SQUEEZING ALL THE young Jedi Knights into Raaba's interstellar skimmer proved to be a challenge, especially with the two large Wookiees. But Lowie did not mind being in such cramped quarters with his friends . . . and Raaba.

The wound in his side still burned, but Raaba had efficiently applied a graft bandage to the injury, finding her well-stocked medikit quickly, as if she had cause to use it with some frequency. She calmly helped the exhausted companions settle into her crowded skimmer, which she had named the *Rising Star*.

Lowie found it very unsettling to see the chocolate-furred young Wookiee woman—a friend whom he had once mourned as dead—now resurrected before him. He

145

kept his eyes on Raaba's glossy coat as she guided the little craft across to the rim of the crater where the *Rock Dragon* waited. She flew with a speed and conscious skill that stopped just this side of recklessness. Her eyes flashed bright, her movements were strong—and she seemed to be avoiding conversation.

Lowie felt a growing discomfort. He wanted to ask Raaba so many questions, find out why she had disappeared, why she hadn't communicated with him for so long. Her loss and apparent death had been one of the saddest experiences in Lowie's life.

"Er, Master Lowbacca, if you would be so kind as to give me a bit more room . . . ," Em Teedee said. Lowie looked down at his waist to find that he was so hunched over in the cramped cockpit that the little droid had been smashed between his stomach and his thigh. Yet somehow Lowie hadn't noticed the discomfort. After he rearranged his lanky limbs to remedy the problem, the little droid sighed. "Ah, thank you, Master Lowbacca. That's much better. Now my systems aren't in danger of overheating."

Circling the broad crater, Raaba brought

her skimmer in for a smart landing fifty meters from the *Rock Dragon*, and the young Jedi Knights gratefully climbed out, stretching their cramped muscles. In the aftermath of their ordeal with the combat arachnids, they all thanked her profusely. Raaba, though, seemed indifferent to the gratitude of the humans.

Jacen and Jaina joked in relief after their near brush with death. Lowie could see curiosity about Raaba on the twins' faces and sensed the questions that clamored to be asked. Tenel Ka's expression was less readable, but he could sense her interest as well.

Raabakyysh straightened her dusty red headband, pushed the ornamented armlets more firmly against her biceps, and gruffly asked if she could do anything else to help.

Jaina's brandy-brown eyes narrowed in a shrewd expression that Lowie knew well. "Yes. Matter of fact, I really need to run a calibration check on the jump sequencer in our hyperdrive," she said. "I'll need Jacen and Tenel Ka to help me—"

A surprised-looking Jacen interrupted. "But Lowie always helps you with—"

Jaina nudged him none too gently with her elbow, and Jacen subsided into conspiratorial silence. "Thing is," she continued, "we're here looking for someone, someone important, and I'm wondering if we overlooked any clues that might help. It would really mean a lot to us if you and Lowie would do one more circuit of the crater rim—just to see if there's anything we missed. And maybe you could do a few flyovers of the crater while you're at it."

"Ah," Tenel Ka said, nodding. "Aha. An excellent plan."

Humans could be much more perceptive than aliens gave them credit for, Lowie reminded himself. He was pleased when Raaba instantly agreed to the arrangement. She seemed happy to help in the search for Bornan Thul—or perhaps she just preferred to be away from the other young Jedi Knights. She made no objection to Lowie's accompanying her, though, and he hoped she wouldn't avoid talking to him once they were alone.

Lowie knew from their past time together that Raaba was not one to stand around once a decision was made. With a few bounding leaps she was back at her skimmer, climbing inside as she tossed a glance behind her at Lowie. He trotted after her, and then settled himself in the *Rising Star*'s copilot seat, a position that had begun to feel natural to him.

With a blast of repulsorjets that sent plumes of dust into the shimmering air, the *Rising Star* lifted off, and Lowie's spirits lifted with it. Through the front viewport he could see Jaina toss him a lighthearted salute before Raaba banked the skimmer and took off in the opposite direction around the rim.

Finally sharing a moment of privacy with her, Lowie felt the growing impact of the good news: Raaba was alive! She had not been torn to pieces by wild animals in the lower levels of Kashyyyk's jungle, or swallowed whole by a deadly syren plant.

But where had she been for so long? And why had she not tried to contact her friends or family to reassure them of her safety? Lowie's sister Sirra had been as distraught as he himself had been. He remembered their terrible months of shared grief.

Lowbacca stared through the skimmer's front viewport for a few minutes, dutifully searching for clues that might lead them to

Bornan Thul . . . and hoping that Raaba would broach these difficult subjects herself.

She did not. In fact, she said nothing to him.

At first he grew irritated that Raaba did not start a conversation. *She* had been the one who disappeared, leaving all of them to mourn. Then, knowing the pain and discomfort her words would necessarily bring, and wondering what excuse she could possibly give, he began to dread what she might say.

Finally, Lowie could no longer remain silent. Clearing his throat with a growl, he began his question in a voice filled with tension. At the same moment, Raaba started to talk. The two Wookiees' words tumbled over each other, merging unintelligibly in the confines of the small cockpit. As each realized the other was speaking, they stopped, waited, began again at the same time—then burst into chuffing laughter at the absurdity of the situation.

With that tension released, Lowie was finally able to ask Raaba what had happened on the night of her disappearance.

Raaba replied in halting tones at first,

averting her eyes. Her yearning to do something important and unusual with her life had been great—so great that she had been willing to risk her life to assure it. Lowie had already known that much.

One night, without telling anyone, Raaba had brashly decided to attempt her rite of passage alone, asking for no help from Lowie or Sirra. But she had no sooner set out from the Wookiee tree city, had barely descended into the reasonably safe upper midlevels of the thick Kashyyyk forest, when a vicious katarn had attacked her.

Immediately, her hopes for completing the mission by herself were ended. Though she managed to drive the katarn away, the beast left its mark on her, tearing a pair of deep gouges along her ribs with its fangs. Raaba knew full well that the scent of blood would bring other nocturnal predator running, ready for an easy meal. To stay in the forest now would be foolish, she realized, and to descend farther would mean certain death. But to go back would mean impossible shame and embarrassment.

Her only hope for survival lay above, in the treetops, in the safe, cozy Wookiee homes where she had lived all her life. Yet even as she hauled herself up branch after branch through sheer determination, Raaba found little hope in the prospect of simply surviving, going back to what had been her routine. Her brave attempt had been an utter failure—even cocky children climbed deeper than she had gone. She had no heart to go back to her friends and family and admit that she had begun her rite of passage only to retreat in cowardice at the first sign of danger.

If was better for them to think her dead. And her death would free her to pursue other dreams. . . .

Raaba and Lowie finished their search around the crater's rim, and the dark-furred Wookiee woman took the *Rising Star* out into the center of the crater, landing it atop another tall building on the pretext of getting the best overall view of the city in the deep rock-walled bowl.

When the two Wookiees climbed out of the craft, Lowie saw that Raaba had brought him to the highest point inside the crater. From the top of the creaking building rose a towering structure made of open metal latticework—a lookout tower or a corroded communications relay, Lowie guessed. Its peak rose more than a hundred meters above the top of the building, level with the distant rim of the crater. Wind whistled through the rusted girders.

Lowie's heart raced at the sheer height of the structure. Without hesitation, Raaba sprang onto the latticework and began to climb. Needing no encouragement, Lowie followed suit.

"Master Lowbacca, do be careful," Em Teedee scolded. "Do I need to remind you that you are injured? You shouldn't be exerting yourself in such a fashion."

Exhilarated at being with Raaba, though, Lowie ignored the pain in his side, careful not to tear loose the graft bandage. Soon he drew even with Raaba as they climbed higher and higher, where their Wookiee instincts told them they would be safe and protected.

After a few minutes he prompted Raaba to continue her story where she had left off.

The feigned death had been a liberating experience for Raaba. Once she had decided that her family would be better off thinking her dead than a failure, a giddy feeling had come over her. If she was truly "dead," she had nothing left to lose. She could start over, become a new person.

She had pressed her supply pack against her stomach to stanch the flow of blood from the injuries the katarn had inflicted. Then, knowing she would travel more easily without it, she left her pack behind as a decoy, in hopes that the bloodstained pack would draw away some of the voracious predators already on her trail. She concentrated only on climbing, climbing, increasing the distance between herself and danger. At the same time, she distanced herself mentally from her home, her friends, everything she had known.

Now, as they climbed the open framework of the rickety tower, Raaba looked over to check the graft bandage covering Lowie's injury from the combat arachnids. Perhaps, Lowie thought, it reminded her of the wound that—as far as her loved ones knew—had cost her her life. . . .

Finally, during that long nighttime ordeal, weak from loss of blood, Raaba had made her way to the hangar platforms on the outskirts of the Wookiee tree city and stowed away on a Talz freighter.

The Talz first mate who found her, tended her wounds, and listened to her story, told Raaba that he knew of someone who could help her in her plight. He had been as good as his word.

The furry white pilot and first mate had taken her directly to Nolaa Tarkona and invited her to join their burgeoning new political movement, the Diversity Alliance.

Lowie absorbed the name of Nolaa Tarkona with great interest. It seemed that the charismatic leader's name came up in conversation more and more frequently, yet he knew little about the Twi'lek woman.

The two Wookiees finally reached the top of the tower and perched themselves comfortably on the creaking metal lattice-work, letting their feet dangle. Lowie relaxed into the sense of peace and safety he always felt when he was up high, as high as the tops of the wroshyr trees on Kashyyyk. His ribs still stung, but he ignored the pain.

Raaba touched Lowie's arm and pointed to a feathered avian that swooped and dove around the tower, snatching iridescent flying insects from the air. Then she continued with her story.

The compassionate, visionary Twi'lek woman, Nolaa Tarkona, had frightened Raaba at first. Her lone twitching head-tail and stern features intimidated the young Wookiee. But Nolaa had asked nothing of her and had seen to it that Raaba had the best of medical attention.

When Raaba was fully recovered, the Twi'lek had offered her a place to stay, a ship of her own, intensive pilot training, and a job flying for the Diversity Alliance and helping to spread the word about the idealistic new movement. The opportunity was everything Raaba had hoped for, and she gratefully accepted. She came to admire Nolaa Tarkona, to identify with her fiery enthusiasm, her single-minded pursuit of her goals.

Day by day Raaba learned more about the atrocities that humans, whether in service to an empire or a republic, inflicted on the alien species of the galaxy—*all* alien species. As Lowie listened uneasily, Raaba described many examples of the torture or enslavement of aliens by humans. She explained how Nolaa Tarkona believed that by banding together, the nonhuman races could put a stop to such practices and protect themselves. In their unity, in their diversity, lay their strength against the oppressors.

Nodding his shaggy head, Lowie agreed that it did sound like a worthy cause, to help the many downtrodden species recover from the damage inflicted by the prejudiced and evil Emperor. He and his friends, Jacen, Jaina, and Tenel Ka had often banded together to fight for an important cause or against a common enemy, he told Raaba, and they had always been stronger together.

Flashing him a dubious look, Raaba pointed out that humans could not always be trusted, and that deception came in many forms.

The remark hurt. Lowie trusted his friends as much as he had always trusted Raaba and Sirra. Brushing down the dark streak of fur over his eyebrow, he asked mildly if letting friends think you were dead—letting them spend months mourning you and grieving for you—was one of the forms that deception came in.

Raaba groaned at the rebuke, admitting

in a pained growl that she had been unfair to Lowie and Sirra and to her own family. She had been reluctant to go back to Kashyyyk, however, until she had made something of herself, something she could be proud of. She wanted to return home successful and triumphant, a Wookiee hero. She refused to be seen as a coward who could not finish what she set out to do.

Now, with her work for the Diversity Alliance, she felt proud of who she had become, and things were changing.

Then her voice sank almost to a whisper and she apologized for leaving Lowie, for all the pain she had caused him.

Lowie nodded mutely and traced a finger along the trimmed fur at Rabba's wrist and knee. He thought of his sister Sirra and how she, too, still felt the pain of a lost friend. He couldn't wait to bring Raaba back home. It would be a fine celebration.

Far below, a pair of avians chased each other through the rusted latticework and darted out the other side. Almost as if she could read his thoughts, Raaba turned her hand palm-upward to grasp Lowie's and assured him that she would no longer hide behind a lie. She had important work to do, important work for the Diversity Alliance, and that required her to stop hiding.

Lowie wondered what Nolaa Tarkona had said to Raaba that could possibly command such devotion.

15

THE WORLD OF Chroma Zed boasted the most spectacular amphitheater facilities Nolaa Tarkona had ever seen.

A broad balcony served as a speaking platform, the absolute center of attention halfway down a sheer cliff face. The balcony podium was bracketed on either side by a bifurcated waterfall—two streams of rushing water that slithered down the cliff to join again in a churning pool far below. Cold, damp spray surrounded the platform, reeking of chemicals. Nolaa would have found the water undrinkable, had she been inclined to try it; so contaminated was the water with natural petroleum from oil seeps, bubbling black pools near the source of the river, that the tumbling falls were coated with a sheen of oil.

Huddled in cliffside galleries, the gathered Chromans watched and listened. Tossing her writhing head-tail over her shoulder, Nolaa scanned the thousands of faces— perhaps tens of thousands—that poked out, while the remainder of the Chroman's bodies hid in the shadows.

They were wormlike humanoids with smooth heads, smooth skin, and webbed hands. They burrowed into mountainsides and chose homes near trickling water to keep themselves perpetually moist. Their eyes were huge and round, their mouths lipless and quivering.

When Nolaa stepped up to the podium to speak to them, the Chromans raised their voices in a thundering, bubbling cheer.

The Empire had enslaved the Chromans as miners, using their natural propensity for burrowing to harvest mineral resources on hellish planets. On each slave world, the Imperials had made a practice of choosing one random Chroman as an example, to ensure the cooperation of the rest. They would drag the unlucky specimen out of the group's damp and comfortable tunnels and then make a great show of fastening the victim onto a sunbaked rock, where it would writhe and desiccate under the heat, oozing protective body slime until all its moisture reserves ran out, leaving only a mummified husk.

Such were the excesses that humans visited upon all alien species, Nolaa Tarkona thought. She bit down hard, grinding her sharpened teeth together.

Before she started her much-anticipated speech, two pale Chromans emerged at the very top of the cliff, near where the tumbling waterfalls plunged over the edge. They carried torches high in their topmost hands, keeping the hot flames as far as possible from their sensitive wet skin. The pair of Chromans squirmed forward to toss the flaming brands onto the oil-slicked water.

The flames caught and traveled quickly. A sheet of fire spread, covering the surface of the water with blazing color. Twin molten banners of glory unfurled as the fiery streams surged down the cliffside to celebrate Nolaa Tarkona, leader of the Diversity Alliance, their most revered speaker.

The flames blazed, the Chromans cheered, and Nolaa raised her voice.

"My esteemed colleagues, my dear

friends, those who have also felt the crushing weight of human persecution—you do me great honor." She was well aware of the spectacular image she must have presented, framed by streams of fire.

"Looking at you all, thinking of the past and what you have suffered, I know how your memories must have left scars on your hearts, on your entire civilization. But it truly saddens me to tell you that your story is not dissimilar to what has happened to my own people, to the Calamarians, to the Bothans, to the Ugnaughts, to the Rodians—to practically every alien species in the galaxy. It makes me weep. But the fire of my anger evaporates all of my tears."

Nolaa fell silent for a moment, respecting the memory of the tortured and the dead.

"And let us not forget the treatment of the Wookiees, enslaved for their brawn and their mechanical abilities; or the Noghri, whose planet was devastated and their people forced to become killers, or the Ithorians, whose verdant and sacred jungles were burned, purely out of spite.

"Too many others of our kindred have

suffered at the hands of the human-loving Empire. We must put a stop to the human reign of terror." Tarkona let her piercing gaze travel around the galleries, making eye contact with individual Chromans whenever possible.

"You know the truth of my words. Over the centuries, humans have brought us sorrow in countless ways."

Shouts and howls of outrage exploded from the gathered Chromans as they vented their frustration at the years of oppression and senseless slaughter.

"And yet—" She waited for them to quiet down enough that she could be heard. "And yet . . . that *very* sorrow has been a harsh and effective teacher. We must remember what we have learned, and *never allow it to happen again!*"

Murmurs of anticipatory excitement rippled through the galleries. Nolaa Tarkona gauged her audience, sensing when they were ready for her to go on.

"Now, humans must come to experience the full extent of our pain . . . and *share* in it. Only in that way can they ever truly understand what they have done. By sharing our sorrows with them, we can lessen those sorrows. Humans must understand in their hearts that we will no longer bow to their aggression."

She filled her voice with all the unwavering fervor of her convictions. Her remaining head-tail thrashed with agitation. "And sharing our knowledge and our strength can lead to release, for all alien species. To freedom from the tyranny of all humans— for all time."

Thousands of Chroman faces leaned forward, hungry for her next words.

"Join me in my Diversity Alliance, and we need *never* fear enslavement again!"

The crowd roared.

Now that she had finished, Nolaa felt her own heart beating with the passion of her belief. She understood the terror of this species, of all oppressed species. She felt their anger, their need for revenge—a revenge that she and the Diversity Alliance could provide . . . if only all races from all species would work together to demand the respect and autonomy that was rightfully theirs. She stared at the crowd, and it seemed to her that the number of worm-like spectators had doubled since she'd begun her speech.

High up on the cliffside, out of view, several Chroman workers operated a dam mechanism that shut off the flow of water to the split streams of the waterfall. The fiery water slowed to a trickle, then stopped as the last feathers of flame fell into the pool below, where they burned themselves out. After a few moments' pause, the workers opened the dams again—this time at full force. Foaming white water stampeded over the edge, still smelling of chemicals.

Nolaa Tarkona raised her clawed hands, and all the Chromans cheered wildly, welcoming her as their savior. She would do her best to live up to that expectation, no matter what it might take.

16

ON THE PLAGUE-RIDDEN colony world of Gammalin, Boba Fett strode from the doorway, extending his blaster as he approached his captive.

Zekk could read no expression on the helmet-encased face, but he sensed a tension and a wariness in the bounty hunter's movements. Fett stalked forward, as dangerous as a tightly coiled spring.

"I recognized your ship as it flew over," Boba Fett said. "You are the one who fired on me in the Alderaan rubble field." He paused. "Few have shot at me and lived."

Zekk knew his own expression must be murky and inscrutable behind the faceplate of his environment suit. "You were trying to kill my friends. I only defended them."

Boba Fett stood straight, as if taken aback. He raised his blaster pistol a little, slightly off target from Zekk. "Then you fired upon me with honor," he said. "Understandable."

Zekk couldn't believe what he was hearing, but through his Force senses he could tell that Fett was sincere. He took a gamble. "I wasn't trying to steal your bounty, you know. I'm a bounty hunter, too," he said boldly. "I'm still in training . . . but I have my first assignment."

"And is your assignment the same as mine?" he said. "To find Bornan Thul? If so, we are rivals."

Zekk chose the safest response, while still answering truthfully. "No, I got my assignment from a three-armed bartender on Borgo Prime. Droq'l told me to find one of his scavengers, Fonterrat, who supposedly came to this colony. Unfortunately, it looks like my lead was a dead end—that is, it looks as if everyone is *dead*."

Fett snapped up his blaster pistol, then holstered it. "Your mission does not conflict with mine. No bounty hunter may kill another on a hunt unless they are direct rivals—Bounty Hunters Creed. I will not harm you."

"Then why did you shoot at me?" Zekk asked. Gradually he lowered his hands from his gesture of surrender.

"Had I truly intended to hit you, I would have succeeded," Boba Fett said.

Zekk shuffled his booted feet, uncomfortable to be surrounded by one deadly bounty hunter and hundreds of unburied colonists killed by some unknown disease. "So . . . do we go our separate ways then? I need to find information about my bounty."

Fett marched up to Zekk. "No. We stay together. There is little enough to search in this town, and either of us might find valuable information."

"Aren't you afraid of catching the plague through your helmet?" Zekk said.

"My sensors indicate that the plague organism has died out," Fett answered. "I deduce that the strain was fast-burning and short-lived." Zekk didn't question the statement. "In any case, my helmet is airtight."

They sought out the spaceport's traffic control tower on the assumption that travel records might help them to unravel the mystery of the last days of Gammalin. Since the turbolifts were inoperable, they climbed the clanging metal steps to the peak of the tower.

Giant windows cut into the walls of the circular chamber alternated with dead gray computer screens that had once displayed flight paths. Three bodies clad in rough uniforms sat slumped on chairs, gray-skinned and covered with the green and blue plague blotches. Imagining the stench of death inside that hot, enclosed chamber, Zekk was glad he had kept his suit helmet on.

Boba Fett nonchalantly yanked a body out of one chair as if it were no more than dirty laundry, then seated himself in front of a terminal. Zekk took his position at another screen, happy to see that the back-up systems and the power grid remained functional. After a rapid search, he began to download the last few files in the log-books.

Silently, Fett searched for details known only to him, while Zekk scanned the ar-rival records for any indication of a visitor named Fonterrat. In the oppressive silence, he turned to the other bounty hunter. "What led you here to this planet?"

"A rumor . . . a hunch . . . a partially restored bit of data from a damaged file."

Given that half the bounty hunters in the galaxy were out searching for Thul now, Zekk figured it was the best answer he could expect. "Well, it looks like I found the record of my target," he said, spotting an arrival document naming Fonterrat.

He played the record, which showed the docking of the scavenger's ship as well as a manifest of its cargo. Zekk was pleased to note that the bartender's ronik shells were still on the list.

Within hours of Fonterrat's arrival, though, the plague had begun to spread through the human colonists on Gamma-lin.

"This last entry," Zekk said, scrolling ahead, "was made just one day later." He punched up the record, and the image of a diseased, disfigured man lurched in front of the recorder. His hands trembled; his skin had a slack and blotchy appearance. Zekk thought he recognized the dead controller Boba Fett had tossed out of a chair only moments before.

"This plague has hit all of us," the man croaked. "Must've come in aboard the ship of that alien trader. *He* brought the plague here."

The dying man sucked in a deep, shuddery breath. "He's not affected by it. He seems to know something about it, though he is without symptoms. We have imprisoned him in our small brig to give us—" He coughed. "To give us time to investigate.

"Crime was rare here on Gammalin. We all worked hard together to make this our home. Now nothing is left to us but death. Everyone is dead. Man, woman, child. I fear . . . I fear there is no one left alive even to feed our plague carrier. Fonterrat . . ." He collapsed onto one elbow, trembling. "Ah. No matter . . . he deserves no less for bringing this total devastation upon us."

The man slumped forward, coughing and wheezing, without turning off the recorder. Zekk fast-forwarded through several minutes of the man's gasping convulsions, and then the log recorder's timer shut it off automatically.

"Fonterrat may still be alive," Zekk said.

"I've got to find the town brig." He turned back toward the metal stairs, and was surprised when Boba Fett followed close behind him, his armored boots clanging on the floor.

After searching through several likely buildings on the silent streets, Zekk finally threw open a door to a small secured facility with bars on its windows. Once inside, he pulled a glowrod from his suit pocket and shone it on the row of makeshift cells, most of them empty. He crept forward, peering from one into another. Small creatures skittered about, tunneling into the ever-present dust that had gathered in the corners.

One human prisoner sprawled out on his bunk, showing the now-familiar symptoms of the plague. "Justice comes in its own time," Boba Fett observed. "No matter what this man's crime was."

Zekk found Fonterrat, dead, in the fourth cell.

Though the alien scavenger had been immune to the strange plague that wiped out the entire human colony, he had not been immune to starvation and neglect. Judging from the information on the log tapes, Fonterrat had been trapped in his cell, without food or water, for more than two weeks.

Zekk worked the controls outside the cell door. They were simple enough, but he used the Force to nudge the code and unlock the security systems. As the door swung open, Zekk stepped in, uneasy with anticipation. His breath echoed in his helmet.

He recognized the small rodentlike alien from the holo the bartender had shown him—big eyes and ears, pointed snout, and fine gray-brown fur across much of his body. In his delicate, stiff hands Fonterrat clutched a message cube. The ACTIVATED light blinked on the top. He had left some sort of final recording.

Boba Fett was there first, grabbing the message cube. "Hey!" Zekk said. "Fonterrat is my bounty. You're interfering with my hunt. Bounty Hunters Creed, remember?"

"Your hunt is concluded," Fett said. "We will both view this message." With a gauntleted finger he punched a button, and a holographic projection appeared in the air above it.

In his cell, the little alien looked miserable and distraught. Fonterrat held the holocube as if he found it difficult to speak, though Zekk imagined he had rehearsed his words over and over again before punching the RECORD button.

"They gave me this message cube to speak any last words to my loved ones." A sniveling little laugh escaped Fonterrat. "Loved ones! If I had any loved ones, I wouldn't have spent my life hopping from one assignment to another for so little pay and so much risk." He moaned softly. "I did not mean to bring this epidemic upon the human colonists of Gammalin—but Nolaa Tarkona did. I see that now. I did not even know my ship carried the plague.

"I gave her two samples of the terrible organism, but I never dreamed she would repay me by planting one on my own ship, in the code-locked chest that held my payment, so that I would spread it to the first human colony I visited. The humans were helpless against the plague. In their efforts to stop it, the colonists incinerated my cargo and burned out the inside of my ship. But it did no good. If Nolaa Tarkona has her way, I fear that annihilating Gammalin will have been merely an exercise. A test case.

"However, I believe she has been foiled, at least for now. I told Bornan Thul, our middleman, the secret of what her cargo held when we made the exchange. I gave him the navicomputer, and he gave me the code to unlock the chest holding the payment the Twi'lek woman gave me in advance." The image of Fonterrat made a rasping sound that must have been meant as a laugh. "She betrayed me. Now he has disappeared, much to Nolaa's outrage. I hope she never finds him."

Fonterrat swallowed several times, as if looking for more words, then switched off the recording.

"What does that mean?" Zekk said.

"It means Fonterrat could have led me to Bornan Thul, my quarry. But now he is dead and useless to me." The bounty hunter did not seem to care about the implications of the message, though he did hesitate, perhaps pondering what Nolaa Tarkona's involvement with the deaths on Gammalin might mean.

Without asking, Zekk took the message cube from Fett's gloved hand. "Mine," he said. "I can use it to prove that I found my bounty, to demonstrate that Fonterrat is dead. The message cube is of no use to you."

Boba Fett stared coldly at him through the visor of his Mandalorian helmet. "The information is of use to me, but I have already heard it. Take the message cube. I hope our paths do not cross again as competitors."

Fett spun about and began to march out of the brig. At the door, he paused, turning his sinister helmet toward Zekk. "It is against my principles to offer information at no charge, but remember this: Never cross Boba Fett." He checked the blaster pistol at his side. "Follow that advice, and you may survive to become a great bounty hunter."

Zekk stood and watched Boba Fett until he was out of sight. Just to be sure he had left no stone unturned in performing his assignment, Zekk located the burned-out husk of Fonterrat's ship and verified that the cargo had indeed been destroyed. Then he slowly returned to the *Lightning Rod*.

17

JACEN WOKE REFRESHED and full of energy, thanks to the comfortable sleeping gear from the *Rock Dragon*. A noticeable tightness in his arms and legs reminded him of yesterday's strenuous activities: the search along the crater rim, the climb down into the ruins—not to mention being chased by giant combat arachnids!

All in a day's work for a young Jedi Knight, he thought with a smile.

Jacen stretched his muscles and enjoyed the freedom of lying outdoors under the stars on an insulfoam mat that was large enough to sleep a full-grown Wookiee. *Wookiee*. With a tingle of alarm he remembered that Lowie and Raaba had still not returned to the *Rock Dragon* by the time the rest of them had decided to turn in the night before.

The two Wookiees had been inseparable during the evening meal and afterward, talking in low unintelligible voices with Em Teedee switched off for privacy. Long after dark, Lowie and Raaba had left for a walk along the crater rim, deep in discussion, catching up on old times. Jacen had worried whether, in their preoccupation with each other, the two might fall prey to some nocturnal hunter. He thought it unlikely, though, since Lowie had his lightsaber and his Jedi senses, and Raaba had a good blaster at her side. *He* sure wouldn't have wanted to tangle with them.

Tenel Ka had dissuaded Jacen from waiting up for Lowie, pointing out that the two friends might choose to stay up all night to relive old memories or to confide in each other. Lowie and Raaba had a lot of things to work out between them, Tenel Ka pointed out, adding that Lowie had the entry code for the security shield whenever he decided to return to the *Rock Dragon*'s campsite.

Jacen sat up, ran both hands through his tousled hair, and looked over at his snoozing sister. "Hey, Captain Jaina—wake up!" he said. "You're missing half the morning."

Pulling down the lightweight blanket under which she had slept, Jaina rolled over on her mat, propped her chin on both fists, and glowered at her twin as she stifled a yawn. "Well . . . ?" she demanded. "I was just considering our options. Deep in thought."

"Uh-huh," Jacen said, not believing her for an instant. "What time do you want me to help you with the preflight check? If there's nothing else we can do here on Kuar, shouldn't we get back to the Jedi academy before Uncle Luke gets too concerned?"

Jaina quirked a skeptical eyebrow at him, then rubbed her eyes. "You're right. Let's do it after the morning meal, in about an hour." Her face disappeared under her blanket again. "Or longer."

Jacen got up and headed for the *Rock Dragon*'s refresher unit. To one side of the ship, wearing a supple lizard-hide exercise outfit, her hair freshly braided, Tenel Ka had already nearly finished her morning calisthenics, taking advantage of the cool shadows. Tiny pearls of perspiration glinted on her bare skin.

He saw no sign of any extra sleeping mats spread out on the ground, and guessed from the evidence that Lowie must not have come back after all. Where, then, had the two Wookiees gone? When he emerged from the refresher unit a moment later, though, Jacen found his sister waiting to use the facilities—and Lowbacca perched on the edge of one of the *Rock Dragon*'s crew berths, blinking sleep from his golden eyes.

Glancing around, Jacen asked, "Where's Raaba? Did she leave early?"

Lowie smoothed a hand over the dark streak on his forehead. He explained that Raaba had felt uncomfortable about staying in a Hapan ship and declined. Instead, she had chosen to spend the night in one of the *Rising Star*'s tiny sleeping compartments.

"You couldn't have been more persuasive?" Jacen asked.

This time Em Teedee spoke up. "Oh no, Master Jacen. I can certainly attest to the fact that he did his utmost to persuade her, but Mistress Raaba was simply adamant.

I'm afraid she has a certain . . . distaste for human company." The droid made a sniffing sound. "I tried to add my own compelling arguments, but Master Lowbacca switched off my speaker. Again."

Jacen couldn't help feeling that something was not quite right. It seemed that Raaba didn't want to be around the companions, and that it might be more than simple embarrassment or uneasiness. What could Em Teedee have meant about her having an aversion to humans? An odd tingling persisted at the back of his mind, but Jacen could not put his finger on what the problem was. For Lowie's sake, he hoped it was nothing too serious.

"Hey, do you mind if I go over to Raaba's ship with you and chat with her for a little while?" Jacen asked. "We didn't get much of a chance to talk last night, and I'd like to get to know your friend a little better." From Lowbacca's enthusiastic reaction, Jacen would have guessed that the young Wookiee considered his suggestion the most brilliant one he had heard in months.

Obviously, Jacen thought as he followed Lowie past Tenel Ka toward Raaba's small skimmer, there was a great deal he still did not understand about Wookiees—or women, for that matter. This made Wookiee women a doubly difficult challenge! At any rate, Jacen intended to do his best to make sure Raaba felt welcome in their company, despite her apparent reservations.

The previous evening, before their meal, Lowie had drawn Jacen, Jaina, and Tenel Ka aside and told them briefly about Raaba's rite of passage and her decision to disappear and let everyone believe she had been killed. Now Jacen wanted to tell her that they understood her need for privacy and that she could trust them.

In the morning light Raaba climbed out of the *Rising Star* and luxuriously raked her fingers through her glossy chocolate fur. She glanced sidelong at Jacen as Lowie presented the young man, putting considerably more detail into the introduction than he had the day before. Lowie praised Jacen's sense of humor, described his love for animals, and commended his skill with a lightsaber. Only the third virtue seemed to make much of an impression on Raabakyysh, and when Lowie paused, Jacen hurried to change the subject.

"So, uh, what actually brings you to Kuar?" he asked. "It's quite a coincidence that you found us here."

Raaba cocked her head slightly to one side, as if this had been an unexpected question. Then she held up both hands, her fingers pressed together, describing an approximate oval. She growled a name.

"Shells?" Jacen asked.

Raaba explained that she had been sent after a shipment of ronik shells. They were a rare commodity which her employer prized highly, but the trader Fonterrat, who had been sent to procure them for Nolaa Tarkona, had disappeared. The trader last confirmed meeting before his disappearance had been here on Kuar. Jacen's mouth fell open as he looked at Lowie.

"Do you realize what this means?" he asked. "That must be the same person that Bornan Thul came here to meet—maybe even to negotiate a trade with. But what would Bornan Thul want with ronik shells? Especially since he was supposed to meet with Nolaa Tarkona, too. I guess he could have planned to use the shells as a kind of bargaining chip." His eyes lit up. "Hey, maybe if we locate that shipment of shells, we'll find another clue about where Raynar's dad went."

Raaba seemed about to reply when Tenel Ka dashed up to get Jacen's attention. "Company," she said, pointing skyward.

At first Jacen could seen nothing but swirling dust around the crater rim, but then he saw a flash of metal the color of tarnished brass high above.

"I heard your shout. What's wrong?" Jaina asked, trotting up to join them. Jacen indicated the approaching ship with a lift of his chin. His sister's eyebrows shot up. "For an out-of-the-way planet, Kuar sure gets a lot of traffic," she observed.

A low growl came from deep in Raaba's throat. Her dark fur seemed to bristle, and she reached for the blaster at her side. Lowie held up a hand, though, asking her to wait and grumbling a comment to himself.

"Why, whatever do you mean, Master Lowbacca?" Em Teedee said with some asperity. "How could you possibly recognize that ship?"

"Didn't think anyone else in the galaxy even knew we were on this dust ball,"

Jaina commented, squinting to get a better look.

"Except Tyko Thul," Tenel Ka said.

"That's his ship all right," Jaina confirmed.

Jacen now recognized its boxy design and unusual color. Soon the ornate craft was close enough for Jacen to see the slightly rotund figure in the cockpit. He felt the tingle again at the back of his neck, only stronger this time. "I've got a bad feeling about this," Jacen said. "First Raaba shows up—and we thought she was dead. Now Tyko Thul is here . . ."

"And we thought *he* was on Mechis III," Jaina finished for him.

Two minutes later Raynar's uncle climbed out of his ship. His moon-round face beamed at the assembled party. "How wonderful to see you all again. So glad I found you. I brought some food. Would you all like to join me for"—he glanced appraisingly at the sky—"morning meal? I'm simply famished. Hyperspace travel really drains me."

"Uh, wait a minute," Jacen said. "Is there some kind of emergency? Didn't you say you had business back on Mechis III?"

"I did, my dear boy—I mean, I do." Tyko began to unpack a mouthwatering array of foods from an enormous food-prep unit. "I was on my way there when I thought to myself, Tyko, you have only one brother—and although no one else may realize it, it's clear he's gotten himself into some sort of financial predicament. If there's anyone who can coax him out of hiding so he can get some help, why, it's you, Tyko. And so, here I am to assist you in your search. It's the least I can do. Family obligations and all that. Besides, those droids back on Mechis III know how to run the show. And if they don't do it properly I can always dismantle them."

"Indeed!" Em Teedee said in a huff. "The very idea!"

"Actually, we were about to leave," Jaina said. "We've pretty much found what we were looking for here."

Tyko's cheeks grew pink and he sputtered. "Why, you can't—I-I've only just arrived. You must allow me to set my mind at rest. Help me look for my brother—*please*, just for today," he urged. "Have you found any clues whatsoever?"

"Yes. Actually, though," Jacen spoke

up, gesturing toward the chocolate-furred Wookiee, "this is Raabakyysh of Kashyyyk. She's a good friend of Lowie's, and she has a bit more searching to do here. Lowie volunteered to help her, didn't you, Lowie?"

Lowie gave a tentative growl of agreement.

Tyko darted a dismissive glance at the two Wookiees. "Splendid, splendid," he said. "It's settled then. We'll spend the day investigating. Shall we eat first? What may I offer you?"

After a sumptuous meal the party split up for one last exploration of the crater and the rim surrounding it. Lowie accompanied Raaba. The two Wookies left together, and Tyko bustled around after Jacen, Jaina, and Tenel Ka, looking busy and interested, though he frequently glanced at his wrist-chronometer. They showed him the tattered sash they had found, along with its dire warning, and told him about the meeting, perhaps with a scavenger named Fonterrat. Otherwise, the day was spent in what proved ultimately to be a fruitless search.

As they gathered for evening meal, however, Tyko Thul seemed satisfied with their efforts. "My only regret is that I still have no idea what kind of shady scheme my brother's gotten himself involved in," he said. "Oh well, it was worth the attempt to look around here. Now I can rest easy."

Jacen felt unaccountably protective of Raynar in the young man's absence. "Raynar believed that his father was completely honorable," he objected. "How can you be so sure he's gotten himself involved in a shady scheme? We don't really have any evidence of that."

Tyko favored him with a condescending smile. "My dear boy, of *course* Bornan's involved in something shady. Why else would he make an appointment with that rabble-rousing firebrand Nolaa Tarkona and then simply disappear? I can't believe he'd even associate with such a despicable troublemaker as that Twi'lek woman. Then again, he's always had bad judgment in selecting business associates, and Tarkona is one of the worst."

Raaba sat up straight at Tyko's comment about Nolaa Tarkona. Her fur bristled, and a growl rumbled deep in her throat.

"No, no, I know my brother," Tyko went on, ignoring the Wookiee. "You mark my words. He's gotten himself into trouble because of the people, or the *things*, with whom he associates."

Angrily, Raaba stood and stalked away into the darkness. Lowie quickly followed her, and Jacen could hear them in the distance, conversing in strained tones. Oblivious to the angry reactions his insults had inspired, Tyko continued talking as if nothing had happened, though Jacen didn't hear a word he said.

Only moments later, with a whine of repulsorjets, Raaba's interstellar skimmer streaked off into the night, vanishing among the stars above.

When Lowie returned to the group, silent and dispirited, Tyko simply shrugged. "A bit hotheaded, isn't she?" he remarked, then dug back into the food packets. "Now, what may I offer you to eat?"

18

LATER ON, AS the night hung dark around them, Jacen looked up into a sky bristling with sharp pinpoints of stars. The broad band of the galaxy's midsection stretched overhead like a pearly river.

He felt the weight of thousands of years of unchronicled history seeping out of Kuar's ruins, ancient mysteries trying to tell their stories. At their isolated encampment, the tiny crackling fire did little more than emphasize the deep blackness of space lurking overhead.

Jacen could barely even see the blocky outlines of the crumbling buildings in the ruins below. Just last night, camping out had seemed fun, despite the adventures that had shown the young Jedi Knights all too clearly what dangers lurked inside the abandoned structures. Tonight, however, an ominous feeling hung in the air.

Lowbacca sat alone, quietly moaning to himself as he touched the graft bandage that covered the wound on his ribs. But Jacen knew the Wookiee's greater pain came from the deep sadness of losing Raaba again. She had disappeared, taken off in her ship—just as she had done before . . . At least this time Lowie didn't believe that the young Wookiee woman had been devoured by a carnivorous syren plant. Raaba was alive but she was still gone.

Before going to bed, Lowie had told Jacen that Raaba had promised to find him again . . . someday. Jacen hoped it would be soon. He felt the deep pain and grief emanating from his Wookiee friend.

Despite the companions' invitation, Tyko Thul had insisted on sleeping inside his own ship. As he left the others, he was clearly in high spirits. He was delighted to have found some inkling of Bornan Thul— though why Raynar's father had come to this isolated place to meet with some scavenger, he could not understand . . .

Tenel Ka had quickly fallen asleep, using

her warrior skills to snatch a moment of rest, storing her energy for whenever she might need it. Jacen could tell by the placement of her supple body, the ever-present tenseness in her limbs, and the rippling muscles beneath her smooth skin that the warrior girl was staying on the edge of full alertness. With only a moment's warning, Tenel Ka would be wide awake again and ready for battle.

Jaina sat next to her twin brother. They both remained silent, comfortable with each other. The glow of the fading campfire splashed around them. Jaina tucked a strand of straight brown hair behind her ear and blew out a long sigh.

Jacen looked into the sky, watching a brief but intense shower of shooting stars. "Look at that," he said, pointing. "It's a meteor storm."

Jaina nodded. "That happens when a planet's orbit crosses the path of an old comet. The leftover debris burns up in the atmosphere, making all those shooting stars." But then she stiffened, squinting as she stared upward. "Wait! Those aren't shooting stars."

The blazing meteors fell in a perfectly

choreographed sequence of parabolic arcs, growing brighter, streaking down across the sky as if under some sort of propulsion system. They left glowing trails in their high-speed descent; sharp deceleration through the atmosphere caused their hulls to glow bright red.

"Those are ships coming in for a landing!"

As soon as Jaina raised her voice to say the words, Tenel Ka snapped out of her slumber. She sprang up from the ground, instinctively landing in her fighting stance. The brilliant, uninvited ships screamed overhead with shock waves of sonic booms so loud they nearly deafened Jacen.

Jaina covered her ears. Lowie roared in frustration. Jacen wondered if perhaps the ships might be Raabakyysh returning with her friends. These vessels were sleek war-craft, though, heavily armed. The pilots appeared to be in attack formation and did not seem interested in making any compromises.

Uncle Tyko scuttled out of his brass-colored ship, shaking his head and blinking his bleary eyes. "What is it? Who is it?" he spluttered, looking up into the sky as the dazzling ships whirled about in long thundering arcs and came around for a second pass. The warcraft streaked back toward the tiny encampment in an assault pattern.

"We are under attack," Tenel Ka said.

As if on cue, heavy blaster fire lanced out to explode in bright puffs when the ships howled past. Blaster bolts gouged molten craters in the ground and set some of the ancient buildings in the crater on fire.

The last two ships in the squadron came in with more specific targets. One blast showered sparks from the starboard engine of the *Rock Dragon*, turning the hull plating to slag and ruining one of the passenger cruiser's stardrives. "No!" Jaina cried, helpless to stop it.

The second attack was far worse, though. With precise targeting from full-powered blasters, the assault ship pummeled Uncle Tyko's transport, bombarding the tarnished-brass ship with irresistible energy until the craft exploded. A long plume of debris and flames spewed from the ruptured fuel pods.

"My ship!" Uncle Tyko wailed. "How am I going to get home now?"

Jaina grabbed his fleshy arm and pulled him along as Jacen sprinted beside her.

"Let's worry about surviving this night first, okay?" Jacen said. "Besides, my sister can fix just about anything."

"Don't get your hopes up," Jaina said, looking back over her shoulder at the flaming mound of debris.

Lowie charged up to join them as they ran for cover, avoiding the smoldering *Rock Dragon* just in case it became another primary target. They all ran toward the ramps that descended into the abandoned stadium, hoping to find shelter there.

The warships decelerated, hovering over the encampment. In midair they disgorged silvery armored figures, not quite humanoid, that leaped out of the craft to drop from a height much greater than any human could have survived.

"Are those armored soldiers?" Jacen asked. "Space troopers in full droid armor?"

"No," Jaina said, "not men in combat armor . . . I think they're *droids*—assassin droids!"

"That means real trouble," Uncle Tyko said. "Run into these tunnels! The droids will have heat-seeking optical sensors to help them locate us, but we need to stay ahead of them any way we can. Move!"

Five of the powerful assassin droids landed on the ground with clanking thuds, their armored legs spread apart, their mechanical arms drawn up in perfect balance. Like automaton soldiers, they engaged their myriad weapons systems and marched forward, led by one droid that towered above all the others . . . It was also much more menacing.

"In here!" Uncle Tyko said, ducking low as he ran through an archway into a crumbling mazelike structure.

Jacen hoped that no vicious nocturnal predators lay inside the shadowy catacombs. Their group could only handle one invincible enemy at a time. They had no choice but to run blindly into the dark.

The squad of assassin droids stopped outside the maze entrance, lined up in ranks, then raised their weapon arms without even bothering to come inside the ruins. The droids fired from where they stood, blasting the exterior walls of the ancient structure. Explosions knocked down columns and support braces. Crumbling stones fell apart in clouds of choking dust.

"Oh, my!" Em Teedee cried. "What *are* we to do?"

"Run," Jaina said. "We're going to run."

The squad of assassin droids lowered their weapon arms and assessed the destruction blazing around them. Then they marched forward in lockstep over the rubble they had just created.

The tallest machine took the lead. His head was long and cylindrical, studded with flashing red optical sensors. The powerful droid moved with mechanical grace, each step an implacable advance toward its target.

"Oh, no—I recognize that one," Uncle Tyko said. "It's *IG-88*—the worst of all the assassin droid bounty hunters! He has some sentience programming and obeys no human orders. We're done for!"

"Indeed?" Em Teedee said. "Quite fascinating. According to my files, IG-88 disappeared long ago, about the time of the Emperor's death. He hasn't been seen since."

"Gee, how'd *we* get so lucky then?" Jacen said. "Too bad he couldn't just have stayed hidden for a little while longer."

"If IG-88 is leading this group of assassin droids, then they won't give up easily," Jaina said.

"This is a fact," Tenel Ka answered. "Even worse—assassin droids rarely miss when they fire their weapons."

The companions dashed deeper into the shadows away from the fallen pillars and walls, searching for a place to hide. The assassin droids marched after them, weapons loaded and drawn, continuing their relentless pursuit.

19

RUNNING INSIDE THE shadowy tunnels, ducking to avoid low-hanging support beams, Jacen found a passageway that led farther downward. He saw fallen debris cluttering the ramp, but the passage seemed to open into a larger chamber underneath, which might offer them a place to hide—or at least to fight.

"This way!" he said, and ran headlong down the sloping passageway.

Hearing Jacen's voice, the assassin droids opened fire again and blasted holes in the ancient walls. Tyko Thul needed no further encouragement and scrambled after Jacen. Jaina, Tenel Ka, and Lowie followed, trying to keep up without running into each other.

They reached the bottom of the ramp, and the midnight darkness of the catacombs became thicker and oilier. The blackness lacked even the faint respite of stars twinkling far overhead. The sluggish air smelled thick and damp, clogged with mildew, as if nothing had ventured down here willingly for hundreds of years. Clouds of dust stirred under their feet as they rushed ahead.

"This is as bad as the spice mines of Kessel," Jacen muttered.

Lowie scraped his ginger-furred head on an overhanging marble archway; Jaina stumbled on the uneven floor. Grumbling in vexation, she pulled out her lightsaber. "I can't see where I'm going!"

Jacen was about to warn his sister not to create so much light, but Jaina ignited the weapon, instantly flooding the surrounding chambers with dazzling electric violet brilliance. She glanced over at her brother and raised her eyebrows. "Those assassin droids can see in the dark anyway—*we're* the only ones who were blinded. No sense making it worse for ourselves."

The companions rushed onward. By the crackling light of his sister's energy sword, Jacen could see that they had entered a broad chamber buried below one of the ancient structures in the crater wall. Portions of the ceiling had fallen all around, but this underground chamber seemed to have many exits, low tunnels that could be hidden lairs for strange, deadly creatures. . . .

In the violet illumination, Jacen spotted glinting eyes and flashing fangs. He swallowed hard. With his Jedi senses he detected skittering movement and the sudden sharp focus of predatory attention. "Blaster bolts!" he said as the young Jedi Knights skidded to a halt, wondering which direction to go next. "Maybe this wasn't such a good hiding place after all."

Before he could worry further, bolts of sizzling light streaked across the room. Flashes of destructive fire spat from high-powered cannons carried by the assassin droids as the machines marched into the chamber where Jacen and his companions had hoped to hide or make their last stand. With a thrumming of metal and a powerful whine of servomotors, the murderous droids attacked. The young Jedi Knights had no place to run.

As one, Tenel Ka, Lowbacca, and Jacen lit their lightsabers and prepared to fight. Tyko Thul stayed beside them, muttering that he wished he had thought to stash a few weapons outside his ship before the droids destroyed it.

IG-88 himself clomped into the musty chamber and fixed his quarry with his flashing scarlet optical sensors. The chief droid swiveled his body core sideways, bringing up his arm and focusing its built-in laser rifle. He targeted on Jacen and fired.

But Jacen reacted in a flash. Flowing with the Force, he brought up his lightsaber blade in the same instant that Tenel Ka reached out to protect him, crossing her turquoise blade with his emerald one. IG-88's deadly bolt struck both lightsabers and ricocheted off, splashing its fire into one of the darkened side tunnels.

A roar of pain exploded from the shadows, and seconds later a mass of jointed legs and flashing eyes and smashing jaws clattered out with a bellow, as if sounding a call for other monsters to join it. The huge combat arachnid launched itself into the fray while other spider beasts stormed out of the surrounding tunnels, disturbed by the battle and hungry for fresh prey.

"Oh dear, not again!" Em Teedee shrilled. "I detest those creatures."

"This was definitely *not* a good idea,"

Uncle Tyko said. His face had turned a pale gray, and he seemed much more concerned about the arachnids than the deadly droids.

"I suggest we discuss the merits of our escape plans *after* we have escaped," Tenel Ka said brusquely.

Except for Uncle Tyko, the companions stood back-to-back to defend each other against the double threat of the assassin droids and the combat arachnids. Clicking their jaws, the hideous creatures roared and skittered forward. The murderous droids fell into formation and brought all their weapons to bear.

IG-88 launched a powerful grenade into the lead combat arachnid. The sharp projectile punctured the spider monster's body armor. The arachnid reared up, squealing in pain and clawed at the wounded side with its sharp forelegs.

Then the grenade exploded, blasting the bloated abdomen into dripping chunks that spattered the stone walls. A pair of twitching, disconnected legs splatted against the far wall.

Enraged, the other combat arachnids boiled forward, hurling themselves indiscriminately at all the targets in the room.

Jacen lashed out with his lightsaber, clipping off a side leg as one of the creatures galloped by. The monster did not even pause, so intent was it on stampeding into the foremost assassin droid.

The burly, durasteel-framed machine gripped the arachnid's legs with powerful hydraulic motivators and ripped the creature limb from limb, as if the action were part of an assembly-line process. But the creature's razor-sharp defenses worked against the droid as well. Mandibles chewed on its domed metal head until the assassin droid's central processor had been ruined.

Finally, the assassin droid's functions ceased and its body seized up, immobilized by the death grip of the mortally wounded combat arachnid. The giant creature sagged in death on top of the broken assassin droid. Both lay still.

One of the relentless droids marched forward, raising its blaster rifle toward Jaina—but she moved too quickly with her lightsaber, severing the weapon's tip. When the droid attempted to fire, the blaster rifle exploded, sending out shrapnel and damaging the droid's optical sensors.

"How's *this* for a system malfunction?" Jaina said, spitting the words out through clenched teeth. She thrust her lightsaber into the droid like a sword, piercing its body core. Sparks flew as its spinal processors were severed. Blinded and immobile, it slumped down.

"Jaina, look out!" Jacen cried, charging in as one of the combat arachnids reared up behind her, ready to pounce. Jaina whirled, jolted out of her victorious reverie.

Jacen chopped with his lightsaber, slashing off the combat arachnid's mandibles and leaving it to drip green ooze from its mouth. "I like animals," he explained unrepentantly, "but not when they try to eat my sister!"

Tenel Ka, right beside him, struck with her weapon, decapitating the monster. It tumbled to the floor like a crashing starship. All of its pointed legs flailed and thrashed with reflex nerves, but the monster was dead, and Jacen didn't have time to worry any more about it.

IG-88 and the two surviving assassin droids seemed to relish the fight with the combat arachnids, as if these monsters

were worthy adversaries, more challeng-
ing than any quarry they had dealt with in
some time.

The chief assassin droid blasted one of
the ferocious monsters repeatedly, aiming
at its major leg joints one at a time until the
creature collapsed, wriggling its severed
limbs, twitching but unable to move itself.
Then IG-88 moved closer and punched his
long metal arm downward like a vertical
battering ram and crushed the monster's
brain with his durasteel-enhanced fist.

Lowbacca fought against a combat arachnid. Locked in his struggle, Lowie could not
see the danger approaching from behind.
Just before Em Teedee wailed a warning,
the Wookiee instinctively lashed backward.
Sweeping the lightsaber around in an arc
behind his waist, Lowie severed an assassin droid's leg at the knee.

The murderous machine tumbled over
to sprawl on the ground. Even so, it did not
end its attack. Instead, hauling out its
blasters, the droid fired low from its prone
position.

Attuned to the Force, Lowbacca leaped
into the air. Blaster bolts peppered the area
where his shaggy legs had been a moment

before and strafed across the combat arachnid Lowie had been fighting. The creature was thrown backward, its bloated crimson body split open.

Landing in between bursts of blaster fire, Lowie whirled around and struck again with his molten bronze lightsaber, cleaving the droid's metallic head and optical sensors cleanly into two sparking halves.

One of the last surviving combat arachnids had seized Tyko Thul with its sharp claws and pointed legs, and now lifted the older man into the air.

"Help me, help me!" he shouted. He flailed and screamed, trying to escape, but Raynar's uncle had no Jedi powers, no lightsaber, not even a blaster.

Jacen turned, as did the other young Jedi Knights, but the first two to respond to the distress call were IG-88 and the remaining assassin droid. The deadly machines lunged forward, heedless of any danger to themselves, as if truly dedicated to saving the older man.

With precise surgical blasts from their laser rifles, they sliced off the arachnid limbs that held Uncle Tyko. The round-faced man tumbled to the floor as the two assassin droids hit the spider monster from both sides, using their brute strength to drive it backward.

IG-88 jammed a small grenade between the creature's clacking mandibles and held it there. The arachnid writhed and spat, drooling poisonous venom from its jaws as it tried to rid itself of the offensive grenade. IG-88 did not release his grip, however, until the bomb detonated. The explosion mangled the droid's durasteel hand . . . but did far worse damage to the combat arachnid, which shuddered and fell dead.

The two remaining creatures squealed and retreated into their dark tunnels. IG-88's bright red optical sensors gleamed in the dimness, seeking other targets. He and the other assassin droid reached down and grasped Uncle Tyko. The brightly robed man, trembling in terror, was unable to resist.

"You are Tyko Thul," IG-88 said, clamping his damaged arm around his captive. "You are my bounty. You are my prisoner. Do not resist."

"Help me!" Uncle Tyko said.

IG-88 looked at Jacen, Jaina, Tenel Ka, and Lowie. "Do not follow—or you will be destroyed. Tyko Thul must remain alive," the assassin droid said, as if in reassurance. "He will not be harmed . . . unless *you* force us to harm him."

The harsh synthesized voice sounded cold and implacable in the enclosed chamber. IG-88 extended his free arm with its built-in blaster rifle. The other assassin droid used both arms to point weapons at the young Jedi Knights, who stood frozen and uncertain.

Then, with uncanny speed, the two droids hustled their captive out of the room and up the steeply sloping ramp, their metal footsteps thundering. Uncle Tyko's despairing wail echoed through the chambers, then faded into the distance.

"Hey, let's go!" Jacen said. "We've got to help Tyko!"

"How?" Jaina asked in anguish. "If we fight, they'll kill him."

"Tyko should not have left the protection of the convoy fleet," Tenel Ka said. "Someone clearly wants Thul hostages. Bornan Thul has disappeared. The traitorous guard on the *Tradewyn* tried to kidnap Raynar and Aryn Dro Thul. And now these droids

have taken Tyko Thul prisoner." She shook
her head. "We should have expected it."

"Let's get out of here," Jacen said.

Lowie gave a discouraged groan. "Indeed yes," Em Teedee said. "I believe this
entire expedition has been an unqualified
disaster."

20

COVERED WITH GRIME and sweat, the somber group of young Jedi Knights set to work the next morning repairing the damaged *Rock Dragon*. Though Tenel Ka's ship carried a generous reserve of spare parts for emergencies, the damage the Hapan passenger cruiser's engines had sustained would require a great deal of time and ingenuity to fix.

Until then, they couldn't get off the isolated planet of Kuar—and IG-88 and the assassin droids still held Tyko Thul hostage. They were stuck.

And so Lowie found himself sifting through the tarnished-brass wreckage of Tyko Thul's ship, searching for engine parts that could be salvaged whole or somehow adapted to the needs of the *Rock Dragon*.

"Why does everyone wish to destroy my ship?" Tenel Ka muttered, examining the upper hull of her damaged ship with a handheld scanner while Jacen crawled underneath to check the lower hull plating. Em Teedee, already hooked to the ship's diagnostic systems, generated a list of the minimum repairs needed to make the passenger shuttle spaceworthy again, just so they could get home.

From the engine compartment, which swallowed her up to her waist, Jaina tracked everyone's progress with a steady flow of questions and answers. Despite the circumstances, the companions found the demands of the repair activities both familiar and comforting. They had been through all of this before.

More than once Lowie found his gaze straying skyward. He was hoping for a glimpse of Raaba's skimmer, the *Rising Star*. But he knew the young Wookiee woman would not be back. She had been too angry last night over Tyko Thul's rudeness and his obvious contempt for Nolaa Tarkona, the Twi'lek political leader Raaba idolized. Lowie had gone after her to calm her down and bring her back—but it had been no use.

When Raaba decided to leave, Lowie had made a last-ditch request of her: that she try to find out the subject of the meeting Nolaa Tarkona was to have had with Bornan Thul. If that mystery could be solved, he'd told her, they could all be happy, human and alien alike.

The suggestion had been a mistake. Raaba had turned her anger on Lowie, furious that he would suggest that she spy on her employer for his human so-called friends. She had stormed off toward her skimmer.

Lowie studied a half-melted chunk of circuitry before discarding it. It could be of no use to the *Rock Dragon*. Lowie might have despaired of ever seeing Raaba again, had it not been for the fact that at the last moment she had hesitated, turned, and told him she would find him some other time—no matter where he went. She would not abandon him entirely, ever again.

Then Raabakyysh was gone, a flash of chocolate-brown fur in the murky shadows of Kuar's night.

Lowie was certain Raaba could have had

nothing to do with the kidnapping of Tyko Thul. None of them had even known the man was coming to Kuar, and she certainly hadn't had time to arrange for his abduction or to summon a band of assassin droids. He comforted himself with the possibility that his friend might get over her anger and send him some information about Nolaa Tarkona after all. She had to know how much it meant to him.

Lowie picked up a chunk of battered brass-colored hull plating and tossed it aside. He gave a roar of triumph. There on the ground lay a fully intact repulsor module that had somehow survived the destruction of Tyko's ship. Thoughts of Raaba were swept aside as Lowie ran to show Jaina his find.

Now that the *Rock Dragon* was finally functional again, Jacen watched with a sense of satisfaction as Kuar dwindled behind them in the viewports. He was glad to finally leave the dusty planet that had caused them so much trouble.

"Next stop, Yavin 4," Jaina said as Lowie prepared the passenger cruiser for its jump to hyperspace.

"By now, Uncle Luke'll be worried about us," Jacen said. "We're already a day late getting back."

"Rest assured, Master Jacen," Em Teedee said. "I've calculated the most expeditious route for our return. We'll be there in a matter of hours." Lowie reached up to the little droid, who sat mounted on the control panel, and gave him a pat.

"Still wish we had some way of contacting Raynar and his parents' fleet," Jaina said. "And I wish we had better news to offer—but the situation has only gotten worse." She sighed, looking out at the stars and thinking about the long distance to home. "Okay, punch it, Lowie."

The *Rock Dragon* made its jump, and hyperspace extruded the stars into glowing lines around them.

Lowie gave a thoughtful rumble. "No, I'm afraid not, Master Lowbacca," Em Teedee said. "I didn't store any of the locations of the Bornaryn fleet's next jumps, lest it result in a security breach. I set the *Tradewyn*'s navicomputers with full randomization along known routes."

Jacen sighed. "And Tyko Thul was our only other contact with the fleet. But Raynar will be back in touch—I doubt he'll stay in hiding for long, because he wants to help so badly." He heaved a sigh. "I don't know about you, but I dread having to tell Raynar that not only didn't we find his father, but we lost his uncle as well."

"These are *not* facts," Tenel Ka said. "We did find evidence of Bornan Thul on Kuar. And Tyko's abduction was beyond our control. It is part of a larger puzzle."

Jacen took some comfort in his friend's words.

"We still don't know where Raynar's father went from Kuar," Jaina said. "We only have a few clues and a lot of galaxy to cover."

"Hey, maybe once we're back on Yavin 4 we can contact Zekk and see if he's run across anything that might help," Jacen suggested. "He wanted to be a bounty hunter, after all."

Jaina nodded, brightening a bit at his words. She longed for an excuse to contact Zekk and still hoped that he might one day come back to them.

Lowie added that he had asked Raabakyysh to send him any information she might learn about Bornan Thul.

"Ah," Tenel Ka said. "Aha. I am glad to know that my own family is safe, with only the intrigues and assassination attempts of the Hapan royal court to concern them."

"I think we should all go to the Great Temple's comm center when we get back to Yavin 4," Jaina said, "and check in with our families." All of the young Jedi Knights voiced their enthusiastic agreement.

"An excellent suggestion," Em Teedee said. "I shall look forward to exchanging code with See-Threepio again."

The young Jedi Knights chuckled at the little droid's comment as the *Rock Dragon* streaked back toward the Jedi academy and the jungle moon.

The only thing they can trust is the Force . . .

YOUNG JEDI KNIGHTS

DELUSIONS OF GRANDEUR

As the search for Raynor Thul's father continues, the young Jedi Knights turn for help to a most unusual— and dangerous—source: the reprogrammed assassin droid IG-88. They think they can keep him under control. But can one of the most feared bounty hunters in the galaxy be trusted?

Turn the page for a special preview of the next book in the STAR WARS: YOUNG JEDI KNIGHTS series:

DELUSIONS OF GRANDEUR

Coming in July from Boulevard Books!

Inside the bustling, hollow asteroid of Borgo Prime, signs along the walkway fluoresced and flickered, leading Zekk back to Shanko's Hive. The dark-haired young man had received his first bounty assignment inside that popular cantina—and he had come back empty-handed.

Zekk rehearsed various ways of telling this to the blue-skinned bartender, Droq'l, who had hired him to find a scavenger and his cargo. But Fonterrat, the missing scavenger, was dead and his cargo of precious ronik shells destroyed. He had no idea how his employer would react to the bad news.

How would Boba Fett have handled this situation? Zekk asked himself. Fett, one of the most respected (and feared) bounty hunters in the galaxy, would waste no energy on lengthy explanations or excuses. Fett would come straight to the point. Zekk decided he would have to do the same.

Tossing his ponytail over his shoulder, Zekk stopped before the entrance to an enormous cone-shaped building with horizontal ridges like smooth circular waves up its sides. He took a brief moment to perform a Jedi relaxation technique, something Master Skywalker had taught him—*not* Brakiss of the Shadow Academy.

Then, projecting all of the confidence a professional bounty hunter ought to feel, Zekk strode into Shanko's Hive.

Air clouded with exotic scents and flavors enveloped him in a pale gray haze. Though the interior of the hive cantina had no flat edges, the contrasting islands of sound and silence, of light and dimness, gave the illusion of dozens of shadowy corners. A quick glance at the bar told Zekk that the insectoid proprietor Shanko had emerged from hibernation and was in no mood to humor fools.

Brief, confident, professional, Zekk reminded himself. His steps did not falter as he walked toward the bar and tossed a credit chit on it. "Osskorn Stout," he said without preamble. "I have business with your bartender."

Dark, foamy ale sloshed onto the counter from the flagon Shanko thunked down in front of him. As Zekk scooped up the tankard to take a gulp, one of Shanko's many glossy arms roughly swept out to mop up the spill while another gave an abrupt jerk, indicating an area to Zekk's right.

Still drinking thirstily, he looked over to see Droq'l in conversation with a patron who stood just outside the circle of light cast by the bar's globelamps. Zekk nodded his thanks, and with renewed confidence he strode toward the three-armed bartender. As if he had an extra eye in the back of his head—which he did, Zekk now recalled—Droq'l turned just as the young bounty hunter approached, tankard in hand.

"Did you find what I sent you for?" the bartender asked, his blue face eager.

"Fonterrat is dead." Zekk reached into his vest pocket and produced the holocube that contained the scavenger's final message.

Droq'l watched the entire holomessage and grimaced, showing his shiny black teeth. "Gammalin, huh?"

Zekk shrugged. "Fonterrat was imprisoned there when the plague hit. The frightened colonists destroyed his ship and burned his cargo, but the sickness swept through the colony. It killed every human."

"Fonterrat wasn't human," the bartender mused, "so he starved alone in prison after those colonists ruined my shipment of shells." A glint of pleasure replaced the disappointment in his eyes. "At least it was a slow, lingering death."

Zekk nodded warily.

Droq'l sighed and spread all three hands in a gesture of resigned acceptance. "Just as well. I might've been tempted to terminate Fonterrat myself for his incompetence."

Then, to Zekk's pleasant surprise, the bartender paid him in full.

"Glad to see a young trainee with some presence of mind," he said. "You finished what I sent you to do, and you had the good sense to bring back proof of it. That's more than I could say for some bounty hunters two or three times your age."

A thoughtful look crept over the bartender's blue-skinned face, and he drummed the fingers of two hands on the bartop. "Come to think of it, I may have another job for you, if you're interested. Got a client who's looking for a bounty hunter, wants someone who's resourceful and trustworthy—but unknown. That might just be you."

"You seem to be a good enough judge of character," Zekk said, crossing his arms over his chest. "After all, you judged *me* correctly."

The bartender chuckled at his bravado. "You'll take the job, then?"

Zekk didn't dare let his excitement show. "Of course. May I speak to him?" He felt a sense of exhilaration. He'd fully expected to come away in disgrace, without pay, after reporting his failure. But now, because of his own sense of honor—something he feared the dark side had stolen from him forever—a new job had dropped right in his lap!

The bartender grinned. "He's pretty particular, even a little skittish—I think he'll want to talk to you himself before you're hired."

Zekk could learn nothing for certain about his prospective employer. Sitting at a low table in the shadow of a staircase that spiraled up the inner wall of Shanko's Hive, Zekk stared at the . . . *creature* in front of him.

"My name is Zekk," he offered. "I hear you need a bounty hunter."

"You come well recommended," the creature replied. "Call me . . . Wary. Master Wary. Yes, that will do."

Zekk shrugged in amusement. "Whatever."

Wary's voice was masculine, but synthesized. His body and arms were engulfed in gray robes and furs that made it impossible even to guess the creature's species or probable shape. He wore a holographic mask set to randomize so that his features changed constantly. A reptilian tail coiled out from beneath the robes and furs, but this could have been part of a disguise. For all Zekk knew, he could be talking to a female Wookiee, a Jawa on stilts, or even his friend Jaina Solo.

The thought of Jaina made him smile again, and he patted his vest pocket in which rested two message packets—one from Jaina and one from old Peckhum; the bartender had found them for Zekk in the general delivery message area behind the bar.

"And who exactly do you want me to find, Master Wary?" Zekk asked, deciding on a direct approach.

Wary looked around, as if to be sure no one was listening in. Zekk glanced unobtrusively toward the nearby tables. A Devaronian played Sabacc with a pair of disreputable-looking spacers; a Ranat consulted a Hutt information broker; a furry white Talz and a hammerheaded Ithorian drank colorful intoxicants and sang duets to the accompaniment of a nine-stringed wrist harp. No one paid any particular attention to him.

"I want you to find a man who's been kidnapped," Wary said beneath his mask. "His name is Tyko Thul."

Zekk's entire attention snapped back to the creature in front of him. "Did you say Tyko *Thul*?"

The holomask blurred and shifted. "Yes, Tyko *Thul*,"

he repeated. "He was recently abducted by several assassin droids. I want you to find him."

"Every other bounty hunter in the galaxy is out looking for *Bornan* Thul," Zekk said. "Are you sure it's Tyko you want?"

Wary nodded. "The two are brothers. I have reason to believe the disappearances are . . . related—just as the two men are."

An interesting twist, Zekk thought. Finding one brother might lead to information about the other. After failing to find Fonterrat, he had intended just to strike out on his own, looking for clues to Bornan Thul, hoping to repair his reputation. But this direct commission was a much better prospect.

"I'll take the assignment," Zekk said. "How much are you paying?"

Wary quoted him a generous figure. "But only if you find him."

Zekk tried not to show his surprise. Wary stood to make a lot more credits than that if Zekk retrieved information that led him to Bornan Thul.

"But that is not all there is to the task," Master Wary cautioned. "I also need you to send a message for me. I have other urgent business to attend to that prevents me from sending it myself. I will give you instructions on how to transmit it." He slid a hololetter packet across the table toward Zekk. "Do not try to listen to the message. It would mean nothing to you."

"That's it?" Zekk accepted the packet and slid it into his vest pocket.

"Not as simple as it would seem," Wary said. "The message is for the Bornaryn fleet. All the ships went into hiding shortly after Bornan Thul's disappearance, and they are impossible to locate."

"How do you expect me to get the message to them?" Zekk asked, a little exasperated.

"I ask only that you broadcast the message to the following locations." He listed several sites along major trading routes, many of which Zekk was already familiar with from his days with the old spacer Peckhum. "I will meet you here again in ten days—to learn of your progress, and to pay you if you have already achieved both of your goals."

Zekk still wasn't sure why Wary would want to send a message to the Bornaryn fleet. Did he hope to flush them out of hiding? To question Thul's employees and family members in hopes of locating him?

Just as Zekk opened his mouth to ask, an explosion erupted at a nearby table. Zekk blinked to see what had happened as a cloud of white smoke billowed outward from where the Talz and the Ithorian had been sitting.

Droq'l bustled up with a disgusted snort, sweeping broken and steaming glasses away. "I told you two not to let your drinks come into contact with each other," he growled in exasperation. "You should know they're chemically incompatible!" With a big paw, the Talz batted at a smoldering patch of its white fur.

Amused, Zekk turned back to the conversation with his new employer—only to find Master Wary gone.

Apparently the assignment was made and the interview had ended. Zekk shrugged. He had his commission, and he knew what to do. He might as well stay to view the new hololetters from Jaina and Peckhum.

Calling Droq'l over, Zekk ordered another Osskorn Stout, drew one of the message packets from his pocket, and slid it into the reader slot on the table in front of him. He waited eagerly for the image of Jaina to appear—then blinked in disappointment.

ENCRYPTION PROPRIETARY
MESSAGE UNREADABLE

Why would Jaina or Peckhum have sent him a message in code that no standard reader could decipher? He realized his mistake as he pulled a second hololetter from the pocket of his vest and then a third.

He had accidentally tried to view the message from Master Wary.

But how could the disguised man expect an encrypted message to get through to the Bornaryn fleet? And how would the fleet read it unless *they* already knew the key?

Perhaps they did, Zekk thought. Maybe this was a code that belonged to the Bornaryn trading company. Wary might be a former employee . . . or even Bornan Thul himself!

As the thought occurred to Zekk, he suddenly saw the truth of it. He felt it in his bones, in the background music of the Force that sang through all things. Master Wary's synthesized voice had held an urgency when he spoke of the need to find Tyko Thul and a tender quality when he spoke about the fleet.

Zekk shook his head to clear it. Bornan Thul had been here, right in front of him!

He jammed the message packets back into his pocket and jumped to his feet just as Droq'l approached carrying a fresh tankard of ale in his middle arm.

"Which way?" Zekk asked, breathless. "Where did he go?"

The bartender didn't pretend he had no idea what Zekk meant. He jerked his head toward a small door beneath the stairway in the wall of Shanko's Hive.

Dashing out into a tiny alleyway, Zekk looked left and right, but saw no sign of his new employer. His heart raced with the realization that he had been less than a meter away from the most sought-after bounty in the galaxy!

Farther down the alley, Zekk was not surprised to find a pile of gray rags and furs along with a prosthetic reptilian tail where Bornan Thul had dumped his disguise.